Inspired Press Limited

www.catherinecoles.com

ISBN: 9798707342332

Editor – Sara Miller

Cover Artist – Sally Clements

MURDER IN THE CHURCHYARD

A 1920s cozy mystery

A Tommy & Evelyn Christie Mystery - Book 3

CATHERINE COLES

About the Author

Catherine Coles has written stories since the day she could form sentences, she can barely believe that making things up in her head classes as work!!

Catherine lives in the north east of England where she shares her home with her children and two spoiled dogs who have no idea they are not human!

Catherine's Cozy Mysteries

Murder at the Manor
Murder at the Village Fete
Murder in the Churchyard
Murder in Belgrave Square – coming April 2021

Catherine's Website

www.catherinecoles.com

"The most difficult thing is the decision to act,
the rest is merely tenacity."
– Amelia Earhart

CONTENTS

Cast of Characters

<u>Main Characters</u>

Tommy Christie – The 7th Earl of Northmoor, former policeman
Evelyn Christie – Policewoman during the Great War, Tommy's wife

<u>The Family</u>

Lady Emily Christie – Tommy's great aunt
Millicent Wilder - Evelyn's sister
Reg Wilder - Millicent's husband

<u>The Villagers</u>

Theodore Mainwaring - The village doctor
Isolde Newley – The village schoolteacher
George Hughes – The owner of the village pub, the Dog & Duck
Annie Hughes – George's wife
Percy Armstrong – Owner of village Post Office/shop
Ellen Armstrong – Percy's long suffering sister
John Capes – The Vicar
Alfred Cross – Church Warden
Violet Cross – Alfred's widowed sister
Leonard Williams – Church Warden
Dorothy Williams – Leonard's wife
Elsie Warren - The church organ player
Albert - The butcher's boy, Nora's beau

The Staff

Wilfred Malton - The butler
Phyllis Chapman - The housekeeper
Jack Partridge – The estate manager
Mary O'Connell - The cook
Walter Davies - Charles's valet
Frank Douglas - Eddie's valet & First Footman
Arthur Brown - Second Footman
Gladys Ferriby - Lady Emily's lady's maid
Doris - Evelyn's maid
Nora - The kitchen maid
Joe Naylor - Gardener

Others

Phillip Newley – Isolde's estranged husband

Chapter One

North Yorkshire, England – January 1922

"How very outdated travelling this way feels these days," Evelyn Christie commented as she looked out of the carriage to the snow covered fields that flew by their carriage in a blur.

"It was very good of Partridge to clear the lane all the way to the village so you are able to attend church." Tommy nodded at their estate manager, who was also driving the team of horses pulling their conveyance. "And even more loyal of him to insist on taking us himself."

"He has been absolutely indispensable since that business with Lillian."

"I should think so too," Aunt Em said. "Most employers would have had no compunction in showing him the door. And most likely without references too."

"I rather think he is trying to make up for his past misdemeanours." Tommy smiled indulgently at his elderly aunt.

Lady Emily Christie was, of course, quite correct. Partridge had acted disgracefully by having an affair with the wife of Tommy's cousin, not to mention the poaching scheme he had going with a dishonest villager. Since that time, Tommy's faith in the other man had been justified. Today was a perfect example. Evelyn had insisted she wanted to attend church in their local village, despite the heavy snowfall overnight. Partridge had been only too willing to make that happen, despite Tommy's own misgivings.

The previous autumn had brought John Capes into the village as the new vicar. As much as Tommy had grown to enjoy the vicar's sermons, he would not have wanted Partridge to go to so much trouble. Evelyn, however, had become increasingly devout as the weeks passed and did not want to miss a single service.

"I'm sure the good Lord will forgive him his many iniquities," Aunt Em said piously.

"You didn't attend church for years until Evelyn and I started attending."

"It was no fun going by myself," she retorted and then flashed a wicked grin his way. "In any event, I previously committed no sins for which I needed forgiveness."

Tommy laughed. "And you have now?"

"That would be telling, my boy." Aunt Em patted his hand. "A lady should never reveal all of her secrets."

"That's correct," Evelyn agreed, though she nodded absent mindedly as though she hadn't really been paying attention to the conversation.

He didn't need to ask what was on her mind, and he would not embarrass her by doing so in front of his aunt. As occupied as Evelyn had been since the village fete the previous autumn with her dogs and duties as the new Lady Northmoor, the thing of most concern to his wife was her desire to give him a child.

Evelyn had spent the war years alone, apart from her house maid, whilst he was abroad with the army. She had enjoyed her relative freedom and independence. When he returned, it had taken some time for them to fall back into the easy, loving relationship they had enjoyed before he had enlisted. It had taken her longer still until she felt ready to increase their family but now, it seemed, simply making that decision had been the simple part.

As they approached the village square, they passed friends, acquaintances, and shop owners on their way to the church at the far end of the village. The village public house, the Dog & Duck, sat directly opposite the lane that led up to the manor house, Hessleham Hall, that had become Tommy's house upon the sudden death of his Uncle Charles five months previously.

Partridge stopped the carriage directly outside the church and came around to help the ladies down. "Be careful, my Lady, the snow is much deeper than you may imagine."

"I am eighty-three years old, Partridge," Aunt Em said imperiously. "I have seen snow before."

Tommy jumped down and winced as the snow on the road came over the top of his wellington boots. Perhaps he should have put his foot down and insisted they stay home that day. They would all have to sit with wet feet during the service.

Despite his aunt's assertions that she had seen snow before, it must have been many years since so much had fallen in their area of North Yorkshire. It wasn't usual for the coastal area to get much more than a light dusting.

Tommy moved around the carriage and lifted Evelyn onto the path outside the church that had been cleared of snow. He squeezed her hand. "Are you alright, darling? You seem very distracted."

"I'm a little worried about Nancy."

"Nancy, why?"

"Oh, Tommy." Evelyn raised a hand and cupped his cheek. "She's having babies very soon. I can't help but be concerned about her."

"Isn't that something you and your mother have had experience of in the past with countless other dogs?"

"Of course," Evelyn smiled indulgently up at him. "But it's not always straightforward. Nancy hasn't had a litter before and she is huge!"

Tommy grinned. "She is rather round."

For the first time since they left Hessleham Hall, Evelyn looked doubtful. "Perhaps I shouldn't have left her."

"We're here now," Tommy said reasonably. "Don't dogs give some sort of sign they are ready to give birth?"

"They do,"

"And she showed none of those signs before we left?"

"No, she didn't." Evelyn shook her head for emphasis.

"Well." Tommy spread his hands out. "Then let us find your sister and enjoy the service. I can't imagine that Nancy would dare to have her puppies without you anyway."

"It doesn't quite work like that!" Evelyn peered into the church. "I don't see Milly. And James is usually charging about like a bull in a china shop. I can't see him either."

Tommy looked behind him. The carriage could not have passed Evelyn's sister and her children without them noticing. James, the eldest, was particularly attention grabbing because of his complete inability to sit still. It was even less likely that Milly was late, she organised her life, and that of her family, with a military style precision.

"Perhaps she needed to rest," he suggested. "She is always so very busy."

Milly had three children and a husband with a demanding job at the local hospital. Tommy didn't want to remind his wife that Milly was also six months pregnant. Perhaps her husband had simply told Milly it would be foolhardy for her to walk through the village with three boisterous children in the heavy snow whilst in a delicate condition.

Isolde Newley, the new village schoolteacher, joined them. "Neither of my admirers is here either," she announced in an overly enthusiastic tone.

"I'm sure Teddy will be busy in the village," Tommy suggested. "There's bound to be a number of bumps and scrapes for him to attend to in this weather."

"Phillip may have slept in," Evelyn suggested.

Isolde laughed, the sound reverberating back off the stone walls of the church. "Drunk too much last night, you mean!"

It was a very difficult situation. Isolde had arrived in the village the previous September to teach at their small village school. She had quickly formed a close friendship with the village doctor, Theodore Mainwaring. However, their relationship had not progressed because Isolde was already married. Phillip, her husband, had recently arrived in Hessleham following release from his latest prison sentence.

"At least we won't be worried about James trying to catch mice in the vestry this week," Evelyn said, with a smile.

"This building is too cold to attract even mice," Aunt Em said with a shudder.

"This is a church, my Lady," the vicar said. "Not a fine country house drawing room. Heat is not required for my flock to be able to listen to God's word."

Tommy smothered a smile as he drew his handkerchief out of his pocket to blow his nose. John Capes was the only person alive he knew who dared to take on his Aunt Em. It was good fun to watch them spar with each other.

The organ started up and everyone hurried to take their seats. Tommy looked back one last time for Milly. Elsie Warren, the organist, nodded at him, her perfectly arranged blonde curls bobbing as she did so.

***

"What the dickens?"

"Oh, goodness!"

Evelyn looked behind her in the direction of the shocked comments. She couldn't see a thing. "What is going on?"

Tommy, who was considerably taller, peered towards the back of the church and then back to Evelyn. "It appears there is someone on the floor."

"We must see if we can help," she said.

"Of course you must," muttered Aunt Em.

Evelyn smiled as she shuffled along the pew and passed by Em. "I am certain it's nothing nefarious. I think we have had our share of murder lately."

"Not for some time," Em quipped. "You're probably about due another one."

A shiver feathered its way down Evelyn's spine. Although Tommy's aunt was not being serious, it did rather seem as though murders had a nasty habit of happening literally on their doorstep.

"I'm sure whoever it is has simply passed out."

Em's voice carried to her as Evelyn made her way to the back of the church. "It certainly won't be because of the heat."

She heard enough snatches of conversation amongst the congregation to work out that it appeared one of the church wardens, Alfred Cross, was the man laid on the stone floor of St Augustus church.

"Seems a very dramatic way to avoid John's sermon," Tommy whispered in her ear.

Evelyn elbowed her husband. "John's sermons are very instructive."

"He appears to be out cold."

"Tommy." Evelyn turned to face him. "You are doing absolutely no good standing there speaking the obvious. Get yourself along to Milly's house and see if Reg is home. If not, you must find Teddy and bring him back here immediately."

Evelyn's brother in law, Reginald Wilder, was a doctor at the local hospital.

As she moved to kneel next to Alfred and try and ascertain what was wrong with him, she was beginning to wish she had stayed home as prickles of unease danced across her skin.

The steady tap of John's cane announced his arrival at the incident. "Do we know what has happened?"

"It doesn't seem that anyone actually saw anything." Evelyn looked around, but most of those who had been standing around Alfred's prone form had now moved away. "His breathing is very regular though. That is a very good thing."

"I shall go next door to the vicarage and bring some blankets," the vicar said.

"Should I go look for the doctor?" Ellen Armstrong asked as she wound a vivid red knitted scarf around her neck.

"Lord Northmoor has already left to do that," her brother, Percy, responded with a slight frown as he shifted nervously from one foot to the other.

Ellen's face flushed as scarlet as her scarf. Evelyn smiled at her. "I wonder if you could fetch smelling salts? Might that be something you have in the shop?"

"Of course," Ellen nodded eagerly. "I shall go at once."

Percy Armstrong owned the local post office. It also doubled as a general shop, and he also dispensed medicines. He had always struck Evelyn as a quite nervous man, with a weak insipid character.

As his sister hurried past them to the door of the church, Percy raised a shoulder toward Evelyn. "She's hopelessly in love with Dr Mainwaring. It's getting quite embarrassing."

Evelyn pressed her lips together. It would not do to involve herself in someone else's business. However, she recalled only too well how Lillian, the wife of Tommy's cousin, had often spoken to her so rudely and how much it had upset her despite her best intentions to ignore the woman.

There wasn't a chance Ellen hadn't heard her brother's thoughtless remark before exiting the church. Evelyn couldn't leave the words bouncing around her head unsaid. "I do not believe it is particularly polite, or necessary, to discuss your sister's romantic life in such a public place."

A look of contrition immediately flickered across Percy's face. "Of course. I'm very sorry if I have upset you, Lady Northmoor."

Evelyn gave a small smile before turning back round to Alfred who was still prone. She hadn't been at all upset by Percy's remarks, and rather thought the shop owner owed the apology to his sister.

"Alfred…Alfred…" Evelyn tapped the man's cheeks gently as she called his name.

"Think I might go and pull him a pint," Annie Hughes suggested. "I'll bet he'll be extremely glad of that when he comes round."

Evelyn nodded, though she couldn't think of anything worse than a pint of beer being thrust towards her as she recovered herself from a fainting spell. Although, in fairness, a generous measure of brandy or a large gin coupled with a stingy splash of tonic often revived all sorts of things when they were at home in Hessleham Hall.

"Oh, my Lady!" A woman cried, tears streaming down her cheeks. "What is wrong with my brother?"

"I'm afraid I do not know." Evelyn sat back on her heels. "My husband has gone to fetch either Dr Wilder or Dr Mainwaring. I'm sure it won't be long before one of them arrives to give your brother assistance."

Evelyn wasn't sure she had ever seen anyone wringing their hands before, but this woman was certainly doing exactly that. Two small children clutched her knees looking every bit as afraid as their mother.

"Is Uncle Alfred dead?" one of them asked.

"I think he's had a funny turn," Evelyn answered. She reached forward and caught hold of the little boy's hand and drew him toward her. "See how his chest is rising and falling? That means your uncle is still breathing and most definitely not dead."

The boy nodded, then shrank back next to his mother again, the expression on his face showing clearly he didn't believe what Evelyn had told him.

She looked around for the other church warden, but couldn't see him anywhere. She addressed the congregation in general. "Could someone go next door to the vicarage and see if Hilda can fetch a cup of tea for Mrs…Alfred's sister, please?"

"I will go." Percy Armstrong stepped forward. His weaselly voice grated on Evelyn's shredded nerves. She nodded, and he rushed off, probably eager to please after his rudeness moments earlier.

"I'm Violet," the nervous woman offered as she sank to the floor next to Evelyn. "Please don't let him die. I lost my husband in the war, I can't lose my brother too."

The woman sobbed harder, and her children joined in.

"Now, children." Isolde Newley dropped a couple of kneelers onto the floor and patted them. "Why don't you sit on these, and off the cold floor. Perhaps if we sing your uncle's favourite hymn it will help us all?"

Evelyn smiled gratefully at her friend. "What a wonderful idea. What does Alfred like best, Violet?"

Violet had just opened her mouth to speak when a shriek sounded from outside.

"He's dead!"

Violet's stared down at her brother in terror and grasped hold of one of his hands. "Oh, Alfred, no! Please don't leave me!"

"Your brother is still alive," Evelyn said gently, placing Violet's other hand on Alfred's chest so she could feel the evidence of his breathing for herself.

"Dead, I tell you!"

"Who is that?" Isolde hissed. "It's upsetting the children once more."

A crash sounded at the entrance to the church and George Hughes, the landlord of the local pub, hurried into the building. "There's so much blood!"

Evelyn could only stare at him in horror. George's hands were covered in blood as red as the scarf around his neck, and he had what could only be described as an extremely deranged look in his eyes.

It seemed that the man on the floor next to her was the very least of Evelyn's concerns—someone was clearly mortally injured outside.

Chapter Two

"George," Evelyn said quietly as she moved towards him. "What is it? What have you seen?"

Her heart thudded wildly as she approached the proprietor of the Dog & Duck. Whilst every part of her hoped George had come across an injured creature, she was certain George would not have reacted so severely to an animal.

George stared at her as though he had no idea who she was. Evelyn could see Isolde moving the children and Violet away from the entrance of the church and now sat in the pew at the rear of the church.

"There's another one!" George moaned, pointing at Alfred who was still laying on the floor. "There's dead men everywhere!"

His voice rose at the end of his sentence. Evelyn tried to shake off the heavy cloak of dismay that had settled across her shoulders. Whilst investigating the murder of the local member of parliament the previous year, she had become aware that George suffered terribly from flashbacks and nightmares following his service in the war. Was it possible he had hurt someone whilst the balance of his mind had been affected?

"George," Evelyn caught hold of his sleeve and gently tugged it, taking his attention away from Alfred and bringing it back to herself. "I'm very worried about you. Are you hurt?"

George blinked then stared down at his hands. They shook and Evelyn could see droplets of blood on the floor caused by the force of his tremors. "Not me. I…"

"Perhaps you can tell me where the injured person is?" Evelyn suggested with way more courage than she felt.

She drew her shoulders back and reminded herself that investigating was one of the reasons she had joined the police force during the war. Now was not the time to act like the weaker, and less able, sex. That was exactly how she had been treated by her superiors. As soon as the war was over, her service had no longer been required.

It rankled her that she still felt a need to prove, if only to herself, that she had been just as qualified to work as a police officer as a man—despite the fact she was a woman.

George stepped backwards and held his hands up in front of his body, palms facing Evelyn. "You mustn't come outside."

"Why not?" she enquired gently.

George shook his head, his eyes now focused on her. "No place for a woman, My Lady. Begging your pardon, but such a sight is not for eyes such as yours."

"George," Evelyn said. "Don't you remember last year when you allowed me to check over poor Ernest Franklin?"

"I should never have let you see such a thing." George shook his head decidedly.

Evelyn took a step towards him. "George, please. I need someone to stay here with the women and children while I go outside and see if there is anything to be done."

"Women and children?" Indecision played across George's features, the tension in his burly shoulders easing as his breathing became more regular.

"Miss Newley, Mr Cross's sister, and her children." Evelyn pointed to where the group now sat. George didn't seem to focus on the other villagers who sat in pews with horrified looks on their faces. "The children are extremely upset because of the blood."

The blood.

What was she thinking of asking George to stay inside the church when he could very well have been the person who had injured whichever poor unfortunate it was outside?

"Make way, make way!" A business like tone sounded from the entrance to the church behind George.

The landlord whirled around and raised his fists, ready for a fight. "You can't come in here!"

"It's the doctor, George."

"Good morning, Reg." Evelyn smiled tremulously. "It seems things have rather escalated since Tommy came to find you."

"Indeed." Reg nodded, looking at George's bloody hands, which were still shaking ferociously.

"Alfred is breathing quite normally," Evelyn said. "I believe your priority should be whoever has bled all over Mr Hughes."

"Quite right." Reg looked at George. "Where is the injured party, man?"

"In the churchyard," he replied. "Sat up against a gravestone. Looks like he's having a rest. Apart from the blood."

"Can you look after things here?" Reg asked Tommy.

"Of course," Tommy said smoothly. "George and I can hold the fort here. You should go and see to whoever it is outside."

"I tried," George said. "I tried to stop the bleeding. But I was too late. I am always too late."

"You did a jolly fine job," Tommy praised George.

"Don't suppose you would listen if I told you that you should wait here with your husband?"

"Absolute not," Evelyn said resolutely. "Lead the way, Reg."

Reg walked out of the church and headed towards the left side of the church. The churchyard was located behind the church. A field separated the churchyard from the turbulent North Sea.

Evelyn trudged through the knee high snow behind her brother in law shuddering as the sea whipped the wind around them. She had always believed people were exaggerating horribly when they said the cold had got into their bones. At that moment, she felt exactly that way, and began to worry if she would ever warm up properly ever again.

"This must be the fellow," Reg said needlessly, there surely couldn't be anyone else bleeding profusely in the churchyard. "It appears that he has had his throat cut by a very sharp implement."

Evelyn gasped as she moved to stand next to Reg.

"I did warn you to stay inside." He glanced her way quickly. "You're not going to pass out, are you?"

"Absolutely not!" Evelyn replied indignantly, almost offended he would suggest such a thing. "My surprise was not the nature of his injuries, but his identity."

"You know him?" Reg shrugged. "He doesn't look familiar to me."

"He has been staying in the village for some weeks now," Evelyn said. "It is Isolde Newley's estranged husband, Phillip."

"I shall have to telephone for the police." Reg put his medical bag on the ground behind him. "Though I'm not sure when they will be able to get here. The village is entirely cut off."

***

Tommy looked at her expectantly when she walked back through the entrance to the church. She stamped her feet in an attempt to get some feeling back into her toes.

"It's Phillip Newley," she whispered so her voice would not carry to the pew where her friend was still entertaining Violet's children.

"Dead?"

"Oh, he's certainly that."

"Annie has taken George back to the pub to get cleaned up." Tommy looked behind her. "Has Reg stayed with the body?"

Evelyn nodded. "We thought that best. I said we'd arrange for a thermos to be taken to him. It is bitterly cold with the wind coming in from the sea and the churchyard is completely exposed. He will end up with hypothermia if he's out there any length of time."

"He said he tried to get to work this morning but that the road is impassable."

"How on earth did Partridge manage it?" Evelyn marvelled.

"He used some old fashioned plough equipment and the horses," Tommy explained. "It would take him days to get all the way through to the main road to York. I think we are stuck here by ourselves for the foreseeable future."

"I was rather afraid of that." Evelyn grimaced. "Stuck in the village with a vicious murderer. This never happened when we lived in Hessleham, it was so sleepy and cosy back then. Now murder seems to seek us out."

"You are right, darling, it is jolly peculiar to say the least. Now, I must get along to the post office and see if the telephone lines are working. If not, perhaps a telegram will get through. We must let the police know what has happened even if they are not able to get to us."

Evelyn glanced at her friend. "I shall break the news to Isolde."

A loud groan came from behind Tommy. They both turned around as Alfred Cross pushed himself into a sitting position. "What is happening?"

"It appears you fainted," Tommy told him. "How are you feeling."

"Very groggy," Alfred answered. "Who is bleeding?"

Tommy frowned. "What do you mean?"

Alfred pointed at the floor, not far from Tommy's feet. "There are drops right there."

"This is going to be a logistical nightmare." Tommy rubbed a hand across his face. "How are we supposed to keep the suspects in one place, preserve the crime scene and the evidence?"

"No one is leaving the village," Evelyn reminded him.

"No, but if we allow everyone to stay in their own homes, we are letting a murderer free in the village. I should hate to feel responsible if…"

Evelyn cut him off. "Stop that right now! You did exactly the same thing when poor Ernest Franklin was killed. The only person responsible for murder is the person who has perpetuated the crime. If the police were here, they would not have the power to insist everyone stay in one place. Not when the pool of suspects is practically the entire village."

"I suppose you are right. We do not even know how long he has been dead."

"Who is dead?" Alfred asked in an overly loud voice, his eyes wide.

"I'm afraid I cannot discuss that with you," Tommy said authoritatively. He clapped his hands loudly. "Everyone, please gather around."

Evelyn moved to stand next to Isolde and squeezed her friend's hand. She looked around. Dr Mainwaring still didn't seem to have turned up during all the commotion. She tried to tell herself it wasn't at all peculiar, he was the village doctor after all. Doctors were very busy people. Especially when narrow country lanes were suddenly covered with two foot of snow.

"There has been an incident," Tommy said. "As a result, I will call the police to the village. All I can say at this point is that everyone should go home, and keep their doors locked. As soon as I have received word from the police as to what should happen next, I shall let people know by visiting."

"There is probably an easier way to communicate," the vicar said.

"I can't imagine the telephone lines are working."

"The church bell." John tapped his cane on the floor. "When you are ready to discuss things further with everyone, we can ring the bell, and everyone should then meet somewhere central."

Tommy nodded. "I suggest we assemble at the pub. It's in the middle of the village and will be a warm and comfortable place for us to congregate."

Conversation erupted the moment Tommy stopped talking. Violet moved to stand next to her brother while Tommy helped him to his feet.

Isolde pulled at Evelyn's hand. "Who is it? I heard Mr Cross say someone is dead."

Evelyn looked over at Tommy and John, then back to Isolde. "Perhaps we should go somewhere private."

"Let us go to the vicarage," John suggested. "It is warm enough in there that even Lady Emily won't have anything to complain about."

"Will there be tea?" Aunt Em enquired.

"As much tea as you can drink," John assured her.

"Then I shall join you."

"I'm sorry to leave you to do this alone," Tommy whispered into Evelyn's ear. "I must make efforts to inform the police. I shall ask Partridge to escort you and Miss Newley to the pub shortly. I don't want to leave George unsupervised any longer than I need to."

"You don't think he did it do you?" Evelyn couldn't contain her surprise.

"I would like to think he didn't." Tommy's lips twisted in consternation. "But he had a goodly amount of blood on him for a chap who has just come across a dead body."

"He said he tried to stem the flow." Evelyn did not want to believe that the man who had seen such horrors during the war had created one now he was home and safe.

"Was it perfectly obvious to a rational person that his life could not be saved?"

Evelyn nodded. "Perfectly."

"Then he has to be the number one suspect, and I shouldn't leave him any longer than I already have."

"If you two have quite finished whispering amongst yourselves," Aunt Em said in a demanding tone. "I should like to sit somewhere comfortable and warm whilst I have a fortifying cup of tea."

Chapter Three

"I suppose I should feel something other than an overwhelming sense of relief." Isolde looked around the group gathered in the vicar's parlour.

"Relief is an acceptable emotion under the circumstances," John said. "However, regardless of how Phillip chose to live his life here on earth, I do believe it would be remiss of us if we didn't offer a small prayer for his salvation."

The group bowed their heads as John offered a few words for a man they had not liked but who had not deserved to die in such a grotesque manner.

"I wish we knew where Teddy was." Isolde played with a necklace as she bit her lip. "I am very concerned that he is nowhere to be found and my husband is laid out dead in the churchyard."

"It does seem rather an unfortunate coincidence," Aunt Em remarked.

Evelyn wished Tommy's aunt wasn't always so very outspoken. There were times when the old saying 'least said, soonest mended' was very apt. "I am sure he is somewhere in the village attending to the sick or infirm."

She repeated what she had been telling herself since the very moment she had realised the dead body was Phillip Newley, but it didn't give her a bit of comfort.

"What is that you have around your neck?"

Isolde lifted a shoulder and gave a little laugh. "Why, it's a just necklace, of course."

The flush in the other woman's cheeks told Evelyn it wasn't *just* a necklace. It was a piece of jewellery of great importance. Isolde hadn't stopped touching it since Evelyn had broken the news of Phillip's murder

"I don't believe I have ever seen it before." Evelyn leaned forward to get a better look.

Isolde tucked it into her blouse and folded her hands in her lap. "It's nothing special."

"My dear." Aunt Em placed her teacup back into the saucer with a soft clink. "If you insist on telling lies, I do think it would be to your advantage if you were more skilled in your efforts."

"Whatever do you mean?"

"Isolde," John said, with a stern note in his voice Evelyn had never heard the vicar use before. "There are four people in this room, and we all know you are being untruthful. The real question is why? Do you not trust us?"

"Of course I trust you." The fingers of Isolde's left hand reached up and found the chain as if of their own accord. "I trust you all implicitly. You are very dear friends."

"Then the only reason I can think of as to why you won't tell us about the necklace is because it has very great personal significance to you."

Isolde nodded and then burst into noisy sobs. "I am so afraid."

Evelyn moved to Isolde's side and knelt beside the other woman's chair. She handed her a clean handkerchief. "Why are you afraid, darling?"

"Perhaps the more pertinent point is: *who* is she afraid of?" Aunt Em chipped in.

"Oh I'm not afraid of anyone, Lady Emily." Isolde shook her head. "I am afraid *for* someone."

"You are afraid for Teddy," Evelyn said simply.

"Yes." Isolde dried her eyes. "It's just that everyone will think he has killed Phillip so we can be together."

"And you think that isn't so?" John asked. "He is the most obvious suspect."

"Teddy doesn't have the type of personality that would lead him to perform such a heinous act."

"Under normal conditions, I would agree," Aunt Em said. "However, these are quite extraordinary circumstances. Nothing stirs up such great passions as a very deep and abiding love."

"This is not a crime of passion." Evelyn sat back in her chair. "It is very crude and functional."

"Oh, I agree, dear." Aunt Em looked at John. "I wonder if we might have more tea?"

"Certainly." The vicar got up to ring the bell pull at the side of the fireplace. "Is everyone warm enough? I can put more coal on the fire if necessary."

A general agreement that they were comfortable passed around the room. John's parlour was small and cosy. It hadn't taken long for the feeling to return to Evelyn's feet. She wished, however, that it would be acceptable for her to take off her wet footwear and stockings so she could put her toes near the roaring fire as she would have done if she still lived in her little cottage in Hessleham.

That, of course, had been back when she had not been Lady Northmoor and before she had the heavy weight of certain expectations on her behaviour. When she had been plain Evelyn Christie, her life had been much simpler. She didn't dislike her current life but she did find it stifling at times.

"What I was trying to say," Aunt Em continued. "But perhaps not clearly, was that when someone is very much in love with a person the depth of their feelings can cause them to do something that is quite unlike their usual character."

"But you can't believe Teddy would do something like this," Isolde protested. Aunt Em did not respond, so Isolde looked at Evelyn. "Do *you* believe it is possible?"

"I would very much like to believe that it is as you say and Teddy's personality is such that he is not capable."

"That's not at all the same thing."

Evelyn sighed. "I know, and I'm sorry I cannot be as sure as you. Aunt Em is right. Very good people are sometimes capable of doing very bad things if they are unable to see an alternative."

Isolde got to her feet. "I don't believe I will take any more tea with people who believe Teddy is capable of cold blooded murder."

She pulled on her coat and headed to the door. Evelyn moved to go after her, but Aunt Em reached out a hand to stop her. "Nothing you say now will remove the hurt of your words. Give her time to come around, and Isolde will realise you are being both honest and reasonable."

Evelyn sank back into her chair feeling desperately sad. "I think I would like to go home now."

Aunt Em perused her intently. "That is the first time you have sounded happy about returning to Hessleham Hall."

"I suppose it is starting to feel like home now," Evelyn agreed. "And, of course, I can't wait to hear what Davey has been up to in my absence."

"Whatever it is." Aunt Em suppressed a shudder. "Let us hope it doesn't involve knocking over hall tables and priceless vases."

Evelyn grimaced. While Nancy, her elder dog was well behaved and never put a paw wrong, Davey was another matter entirely. It didn't seem to matter what training methods Evelyn used, the puppy remained stubbornly wilful.

Hilda popped her head around the door. "Yes?"

"I was going to ask for more tea. However, Lady Emily and Lady Northmoor are ready to leave now."

The woman made a snorting noise and left the room. When she did not reappear within a few moments, it seemed she had not gone to fetch their coats.

"That woman is quite unsatisfactory," Aunt Em said. "You should really give serious consideration to replacing her."

"I think she came with the vicarage," John replied helplessly. "She isn't all that bad really."

"You are too nice for your own good, vicar." Evelyn rested a hand on John's shoulder. "No, don't get up, we can see ourselves out."

"Speak for yourself!"

"Come along, Aunt Em, I am more than capable of helping you into your coat. Let's go home and have a pre lunch gin."

"That, my dear," Em replied. "Is the most sensible thing you have said for quite some time."

***

"Do you think we should have just left like that?" Aunt Em asked when they were finally sitting in the drawing room of Hessleham Hall with clean, dry clothes, a lap rug and a gin in hand.

"Without speaking to Tommy?" Evelyn twisted her mouth. "He'll probably be a little bit cross with me, but I didn't want to stay there a minute longer."

"I thought you liked murder and mayhem?" Em gave her a sidelong glance.

"I like the puzzle of it," Evelyn paused over her answer. "But the human aspect of it is very unpleasant."

"Do excuse me for asking an impertinent question, dear."

Evelyn raised her eyebrows toward Aunt Em. It must truly be impolite if Em was excusing herself before putting it into words. "Go on."

"I wondered if perhaps you were concerned about putting a little heir at risk and that is why, more so than usual, you feel unsafe?"

"I am afraid not." Evelyn looked directly at the old woman, who she had become very close to but in whom she did not confide. Em came from a very different era than Evelyn with ideals and values that Evelyn, as a modern woman, found difficult to comprehend. "I rather feel that Tommy and I are destined to be childless just like Eddie and Lillian."

"That may well turn out to be the only thing you have in common with that pair. Though I do hope, for both of your sakes, that it isn't so."

"Do you?" Evelyn asked. "Why?"

Aunt Em finished her drink and placed the tumbler on the table next to her. "Tommy desperately wants a child, and I fear you are putting too much pressure on yourself because of that. You have been most unlike your normal ebullient self these last few weeks."

Evelyn's throat tightened and she blinked away tears. She had not been aware that her sadness had been so obvious. "I wish I hadn't been quite so silly when Tommy returned home from the war."

"Do you want to talk about this, dear? You really don't have to. You answered my question. I would not want you to feel uncomfortable, and I can see that you are distressed." Em reached over and patted Evelyn's hand.

Tommy's aunt was right, Evelyn didn't really want to talk about how she had insisted in the early days of their marriage that she didn't want to have a child until Tommy returned home safe.

On Tommy's return to Hessleham, he had been in poor health. When he was recovered, Evelyn had been so convinced that she would make a terrible parent—like her own mother—she had again put off having children. Now she was ready, it seemed that mother nature wasn't in any hurry to give her what her heart desired the most.

"I'm being rather foolish." Evelyn got to her feet. "Let me replenish our glasses and then we will see if we can solve this murder between us before Tommy gets home."

Em glanced at the clock. "Is it wise to get tiddly at this time of the day?"

"It's never stopped you before," Evelyn retorted. She held the bottle over Em's glass. "Shall I ring for a tea tray for you instead?"

"Absolutely not." Em waited until Evelyn passed her glass over before speaking again. "Though we should not make this a habit."

Evelyn nodded to show she had heard the slight rebuke in Em's words. She was right. It wouldn't do to focus so completely on what she wanted that she neglected both the people and duties that were expected of her.

"Now." Evelyn held up the fingers on her left hand. "Number one: we do not know when the victim died. However, there were deep impressions in the snow that made similar marks to those made by mine and Reg's footsteps."

"So you think Phillip was killed this morning?"

Evelyn nodded. "Yes. I think if it had been last night, snow would have started to fill in the hollows. And, I apologise, this bit might be a bit gruesome."

Em waved a hand in the air. "Do go on, dear. I think by now you know I have a very strong constitution and am not likely to have a fit of the vapours like Alfred Cross."

"If he had been dead for any length of time, the blood would have started freezing, but that had not happened."

"Do you think someone who was out fetching things for Mr Cross could have bumped Phillip off?"

"That is very possible, but I don't think we can rule out someone did it before church and then slipped inside."

Em shook her head. "Unlikely. The entire village usually turns out for morning worship. The chances of the murderer being spotted coming around the side of the church would have been high."

Evelyn took a sip of her drink. "So you think it must be someone who either didn't attend church, or who slipped out?"

"I think that makes most sense. What else?"

"Number two: who had a motive for killing Phillip?"

Em sniggered. "It would be easier to list who did not. He wasn't a very likeable fellow."

"No, he wasn't. But some stand out as suspects more than most."

"Teddy is the most likely because of his adoration for Isolde. That man seemed destined to be a bachelor until Isolde swept into our peaceful little village and turned his life upside down."

"She did rather." Evelyn nodded. "Why do you think that was?"

"He was a rather awkward individual," Em said. "But Isolde brought him out of himself. His feelings for her allowed the rest of us to see what had been there all along: an extremely kind, and rather amusing man."

"Whoever would have thought we would refer to Theodore Mainwaring in those terms?" Evelyn laughed. "I remember the first time I had spent any amount of time with him was when Charles became ill over dinner. Poor Dr Mainwaring looked positively terrified."

"Charles had that effect on most people."

"And that is why you suggested that the very depth of his feelings for Isolde might explain why he could have done something entirely out of character and killed Phillip?"

"Yes." Em looked directly at Evelyn. "Once one has become a different person, because of love, they will not wish to go back to being who they were before. Do you see that?"

"And if Teddy felt there was a chance of losing Isolde, he might have been driven to do something extreme?"

"Indeed. Now, who else had a very good motive?"

"Village gossip is that he had a falling out with Alfred Cross in the pub one evening. Percy Armstrong accused Phillip of trying to pass a fraudulent bank note, and I believe the vicar thought him guilty of lifting money from the collection plate."

Em tutted. "That is quite shameful."

"Those are the only events I know of. I am sure Hessleham being what it is, there will be a good many other things that have gone on."

"And now you wish you were back in the village talking this over with Tommy and starting to make sense of the mystery?"

Evelyn bit her lip in consternation. "I do a bit, yes."

"Tomorrow is soon enough for that. You can't ask Partridge to take you back again today."

"No, that would be jolly unfair, and I do want to spend some time with Nancy and Davey after luncheon. Can you think of anything else?"

"I did see something very curious, but I'm not sure at all that it means anything."

"In my experience, it is often very innocuous things that we think are irrelevant that turn out to be the key to the whole mystery."

"When Alfred was on the floor and everyone was focused on him, I saw something very strange. The organist, Elsie Warren, had her hat on."

"In church?"

"I'm sure she didn't have it on when we arrived, but there she was, standing at the back of the church with it on and looking very flustered."

"Flustered?"

"Red in the face."

"Like she had been running?"

"I shouldn't think so." Em shook her head. "Not in the shoes that young woman wears. I rather imagine she was doing something else that would make her flushed."

"Goodness, and in church."

"She had her hat on," Em reminded Evelyn. "So I think she had been outside during one of the readings, or at some other time that she wasn't required to be seated at the organ. I'm sure she had thought she would slip back in unobtrusively, but she could not have known Mr Cross was going to take a funny turn."

"I don't believe she can have committed the murder." Evelyn decided. "You're right, she would not have been able to reach the area where Phillip was found in the high heeled shoes she favours. But both she and the young man she was with could have seen something vital."

Em sighed. "You're going to make that poor man take you back down to the village, aren't you?"

Evelyn nodded grimly. "It would be wrong of me not to share what I know immediately with Tommy. If the murderer is aware they may have been seen, Elsie and her young man could be in great danger."

Chapter Four

Evelyn had gone to explain to Partridge herself the reason she wanted to go back into the village. He told her it was no trouble, he was intending to go back mid afternoon to see if Lord Northmoor wanted to return to the manor.

She decided to visit the kitchen whilst Partridge hitched the horses to the carriage.

"Oh, My Lady!" Mrs O'Connell, the cook, put a hand on her chest as Evelyn walked in. "Was luncheon not to your liking?"

"You worry too much," Evelyn told the plump Irish lady who ran their kitchen. "As usual, the food was delicious."

"It's just there was a lot left," the white haired lady said doubtfully.

"Lord Northmoor stayed in the village." Evelyn sat in the chair opposite the cook. "And after this morning's events, I fear Lady Emily and I did not have our usual robust appetites."

"Quite."

"Are you talking about the murder?" Nora, the kitchen maid asked, unable to keep the excitement from her voice.

"We are not," Cook answered in a stern voice. However, both Nora and Evelyn were well accustomed to the other woman. Her bark was worse than her bite, and she was very fond of Nora.

"May we start then?"

"Nora! Whatever will Lady Northmoor think? She will come to believe all we do down here in the kitchen is gossip."

"Speaking of gossip…"

Evelyn turned to the young girl. "You know something, don't you?"

"About that murdered fellow?"

"Yes, I do."

"Well then you must sit down and tell me all you know, so when I go back to the village I can share what you tell me with Lord Northmoor."

"You're going back?" the cook enquired. "Whatever shall I do about dinner?"

Evelyn thought for a moment. "I rather think Tommy will want to stay in the village tonight. I shall come back, but I do not know yet if I will be back in time for dinner."

"Then I will make up a hamper." Mrs O'Connell got to her feet and put her hands on ample hips. "Nora, fetch the hamper…the large one. Once our hands are busy filling it for his lordship, you can let your chin wag to your heart's content."

When the hamper had been placed in the middle of the kitchen table and Cook had started fetching food from the larder, she nodded at Nora. "Now you may tell your tale."

"You know how as Albert delivers all over the village?"

"Get on with the information Lady Northmoor needs, girl, she doesn't have all day."

Evelyn smiled. She was, by now, accustomed to Nora stretching out her story to give the most dramatic effect. "Yes, dear, the butcher sends him all over the village and surrounding farmland."

"My Albert sees a lot of things, but he would never dream of repeating what he sees or hears." The young girl flushed as she said her beau's name.

"He must be telling someone," the cook retorted. "Otherwise how have you got this information."

"Well, of course he tells me." Nora placed an entire apple pie into the hamper. "He knows I can be trusted. Now that we are officially courting and all."

"I still say you're a bit young for that." Mrs O'Connell shook her head. "Just see you don't let that boy distract you from your work."

"Oh, I would never do that. I love working here at the manor. Albert says when we're married he will let me continue working here because I like it so much. Isn't he the most…"

"Lady Northmoor is growing roots she's been standing there so long waiting for you to get to the point."

Nora laughed. "I can't help myself. Whenever I talk about Albert, everything else just goes right out of my mind."

"I feel the same way about Lord Northmoor," Evelyn confided. "He still makes my heart flutter in such a way that I can't catch my breath properly."

Nora clutched her chest. "That's how I feel. Oh, it's so romantic!"

"We are very lucky indeed. Now, is your information something that Albert has seen or heard?"

"A bit of both, My Lady." Nora added utensils to the hamper. "When he was out delivering just before Christmas, he saw the dead fellow with Mrs Rogers. That is Violet Cross, as was."

"Alfred Cross's sister was with Phillip Newley?" Evelyn clarified.

Nora's cheeks reddened. "Yes, and they were in a clinch."

"Goodness." Evelyn shook her head. "That is shocking behaviour for a married man."

"Everyone knows the doctor is in love with Mrs Newley, but they would never do such a thing. They have more...decorum."

Evelyn leaned into the hamper to hide a smile. "I do hope that is right. It wouldn't do for there to be any negative talk about the doctor and Mrs Newley."

Nora put her head on one side. "I suppose they can court properly like now, can't they? I expect Mrs Newley will be very happy. She's looked so sad since that rotten fellow turned up in the village."

"Rotten fellow?"

"He's not made himself very popular with anyone."

"I did hear he had argued with Alfred in the pub, and Mr Armstrong said he tried to pass a bank note that was clearly not genuine."

"Maybe Alfred wasn't very happy that Mr Newley was leading his sister up the garden path," Nora mused.

"Do you think he was? Could he not have been serious about her?"

Nora made a sound of derision. "Not that vagabond."

The cook laughed out loud. "Where do you find these words from, girl?"

"He is though, isn't he, My Lady?"

"Indeed, Nora." Evelyn fought to keep a straight face. "Now why do you think he was toying with Violet Rogers' affections?"

"He was begging Mrs Newley to take him back. Everyone knew that. He didn't wait until a private moment, he spoke to her about their marriage whenever he came across her in the village. Mr Armstrong had to ask Mrs Newley to leave the shop one afternoon because that husband of hers was going on in front of his customers."

"Goodness, Nora, you do know rather a lot."

Nora leaned forward. "Albert does hear the butcher's wife gossiping to her friends a lot. Now there is a woman who knows *everything* about everyone in the village."

"Do you think she would talk to me?"

"Oh no, My Lady." Nora shook her head. "She would never repeat idle village talk to a person such as you."

"I think I'm quite glad," Evelyn said conspiratorially. "That means we can carry on our little talks. I should miss them if the butcher's wife started talking to me directly."

Nora smiled back. "You said back when the old earl died that you wanted to be friends with us down here. And friends help each other out."

"Is there anything else you can tell me before Partridge comes to fetch me?"

Nora slapped a hand to her forehead. "Well that is what Albert saw. As to what he heard, he has overhead the butcher's wife talking with her friends about a number of women in the village Mr Newley was trying it on with. They didn't know about Violet Rogers, and my Albert wasn't about to dirty her name by repeating what he saw."

"Quite right," Evelyn agreed. "I believe she is a war widow, it would be a terrible scandal if people were aware she was mixed up with Mr Newley and then he turned up dead."

"I don't suppose her brother could have done it? Thinking he was protecting her honour, and all that?"

"I wouldn't think so. He fainted cold between the first and second readings." Evelyn considered the possibility for a moment. "I don't think he would have had the opportunity."

"Quite the mystery." The cook shot Evelyn a sly look. "They do seem to land in your lap with alarming regularity, My Lady."

"It is our duty to solve this murder," Evelyn said primly. "The police are not able to get through. Snowfall has cut the village off. Lord Northmoor was trying to alert them to the situation, but I left before finding out whether the telephone lines were working."

"Ours are down," Mrs O'Connell said. "I heard Mrs Chapman talking to Malton about that earlier."

"Perhaps he has had better luck sending a telegram." Evelyn looked out of the window as Partridge approached the back door. "I must get back to His Lordship. Thank you very much for the hamper, Mrs O'Connell, it was exceedingly kind of you."

"Do be careful, My Lady." Nora bit her lip.

"Whatever do you mean?" Evelyn put a hand on the girl's shoulder.

"I feel quite fearful when you are wandering about after a murderer." Nora looked away as though she was embarrassed.

"It is very sweet of you to worry about me," Evelyn said gently. "I shall promise to stay close to Lord Northmoor. Will that ease your fears?"

"Somewhat." Nora did not look convinced. "Now we're friends, and all, I can't help my concern. I'm the same with everyone I care about."

Evelyn did not miss the cook trying to kick Nora under the legs of the chair that separated them. She was doubtless bothered that the girl was completely overstepping her boundaries.

It didn't take Evelyn more than a few seconds to decide what to do—propriety wasn't always all it was cracked up to be in her opinion. She pulled Nora into a quick hug. "You are a very lovely girl, and I thank you for your concern. I shall come and see you in the morning so you can see for yourself that I am quite safe."

Mrs O'Connell opened the door for Partridge and muttered, none too quietly. "Get this hamper into the carriage and her Ladyship into the village before Nora starts sobbing all over her. I've never seen the like before in all of my years. And her nothing but a kitchen maid!"

Partridge frowned in confusion at the cook's outburst, but simply hefted the hamper with strong arms. "I shall bring the carriage to the front door, My Lady."

***

"Where have you been?" Tommy asked worriedly. "I've been quite frantic."

"I thought you were a detective," Evelyn answered with a cheeky grin. "Couldn't you work it out?

"The carriage was no longer in the street, so I assumed you went home, yet now you are back. I had visions of you making Partridge drive you all the way to York to fetch Detective Inspector Andrews."

"Absolutely not." Evelyn squeezed his hand. "I have complete faith that the two of us will uncover the murderer, as we usually do."

"When I realised you had left, I rather felt you had a crisis of confidence."

"In you?" Evelyn smiled up at Tommy. "Never."

"Ah." Tommy led Evelyn over to a table in the corner of the pub. "That must mean your lack of conviction was in yourself."

"I said some things that made Isolde rather cross with me." Evelyn sat in one of the vacant seats, as Tommy took the chair opposite her. "I think I just wanted to go home and lick my wounds for a bit."

"There was a time when you would have rather stayed in the village than return to Hessleham Hall under any circumstances. Does that mean you are getting used to the old place?"

Evelyn didn't hesitate before answering. "Yes, I am. Aunt Em said something similar to me, about the manor finally feeling more like a home to me."

"I'm jolly glad about that," Tommy said. "It is going to be our home for a great many years to come."

"Shall we speak with suspects and witnesses here rather than in their own homes? What is the plan?"

"As I am sure you have guessed, the police are not able to get through. The telephone lines are not working in the village, but I was able to get a telegram through. The official word is that we are not to meddle, but I am to keep the villagers safe."

"That's ridiculous." Evelyn shook her head. "You cannot guarantee the safety of everyone in the village. Especially without finding out who the murderer is. The sooner we identify the culprit, the sooner everyone is out of danger."

"That's absolutely the way I see it. Now, what do you have to tell me?"

Evelyn related the conversation she'd had with both Aunt Em and with Nora. She also told Tommy that she had arranged for Partridge to put the hamper in the pub kitchen.

"I'm famished." Tommy rubbed his stomach. "If Mrs O'Connell has put some of her world famous pork pie in the hamper, I think I shall have a piece of that before we start talking to witnesses. We should speak to Elsie first, I believe."

"I agree." Evelyn inclined her head slightly. "Where is George?"

"Reg gave him something to help him sleep. Annie is sitting with him in case he should be distressed again when he wakes. Now, let us see if

46

there is pork pie in that hamper and we will go visit Miss Elsie Warren."

"That does seem safer than fetching people here."

"I thought about that when you previously asked." Tommy put out his hands to help Evelyn from her seat. "If I went to collect each person in turn, that would leave you here alone and I do not wish to take that risk with your safety."

"Partridge is about. I believe he was looking for somewhere to stable the horse and then he will come here."

Tommy reached down and kissed Evelyn's brow. "Partridge has been very loyal these last months, but I would rather keep you right by my side."

They went into the kitchen and Tommy piled a plate high with food. "I wish we knew where Teddy was. I would feel so much happier if I could be certain he wasn't mixed up in all of this somehow."

"Come and sit back down darling, there is something else I should have told you the moment you came back. Please forgive me for not telling you before now."

Evelyn frowned. "You're worrying me."

The sat back at the table and Tommy held both of Evelyn's hands in his own. "Now, this news concerns Milly, too. But you're not to start worrying."

Evelyn pulled her hands free. "How can I not worry when you tell me the doctor's disappearance has something to do with my sister!"

"That's just it," Tommy said. "Teddy hasn't disappeared. He's with Milly. At least, he *was* with Milly."

"I think you had better start at the beginning." Evelyn was aware her tone was snippy, but she could not believe Tommy had held this information back—even accidentally.

"When I went to get Reg, he told me Teddy was there in the house. Milly had asked Reg to summon the doctor."

"Why would she do that?" Evelyn shook her head in confusion.

Tommy grinned wryly. "Apparently Milly does not wish her husband to attend to her…um…personal care with regards to the baby."

It took Evelyn a moment to work out what Tommy meant. "Dr Mainwaring had to examine Milly? Is there something wrong with the baby?"

Tommy held up his hands in a placating gesture at Evelyn's heated words. "Everything is fine. Reg told me Milly hadn't felt the baby move for some time and was concerned. Teddy checked her over and mother and baby are both fine. However, he advised Milly that she must rest more, and allow Ethel to take over more duties in the house— especially with the children."

"Maybe we should offer to take James with us for a few days," Evelyn mused.

"I think that is a very fine idea. Now, perhaps we should concentrate on this puzzle in front of us. As soon as that is solved, I'm sure our little nephew would love to spend time with us at the manor."

"You do know James is likely to slide down the bannister and get up to all sorts of mischief that will make Malton want to tear out his hair?"

"I think Malton has been gently eased into life with a young child by that very naughty puppy of yours." Tommy teased.

Evelyn laughed. "You're probably right. I would still like to see Milly for myself at some point today."

"Of course you do. We shall fit that into our timetable of witness interrogation."

"You are certain Teddy could not have committed the murder?"

"Ah, no." Tommy shook his head. "Teddy was with Milly this morning and that is why neither of them were at church. However, he could have arranged to meet Phillip earlier and committed the deed then."

"We are agreed it was sometime today?"

"The prints at the rear of the church seem to suggest the murder happened after the snow stopped falling."

Evelyn clapped a hand over her mouth. "Goodness! Is Reg still out there with the body?"

"No, the police telegrammed to say that, in the circumstances, we could not leave the body out in the open. Normally, as we are aware, they would advise against a murder victim being moved."

"Where is he now?"

"Reg and I wrapped him in a blanket and moved him into the church. John has locked the doors. That was the best we could do."

"It doesn't seem quite right." Evelyn looked over at Tommy, who was steadily working his way through his lunch while keeping up conversation with her. "I know he was rather horrid, but it's all rather undignified isn't it?"

"Unfortunately, yes." Tommy cut a piece of cold meat and popped it into his mouth. He chewed before speaking again. "Reg assures me that a wound such as the one Phillip sustained would have led to a quick death so that is at least one good thing. I don't know why anyone would prop him up against a headstone though, that's jolly macabre."

"They could have buried him in the snow. He wouldn't have been found until it melted."

"It's almost like whoever it was is proud of what he's done."

Evelyn shivered. "What a positively dreadful thought."

Chapter Five

"Let us go visit Miss Warren," Tommy said after he had tidied away his plate. "She lives with her parents, I believe?"

"Not far from the vicarage. I think that is how she got the temporary job with John when Hilda was called away to care for a sick relative."

"I'd forgotten she did that, I'm so accustomed to seeing her at the organ on a Sunday." Tommy held open the door to the pub for Evelyn and they headed outside into the deserted village.

Although the snow had stopped falling, the conditions were still treacherous. He placed an arm around Evelyn's shoulders to keep her steady.

"I think John was lost without Elsie's organisation, polite demeanour, and efficiency when Hilda returned. I'm not sure he knows what to do with that person. She's quite rude. I thought Aunt Em was going to pitch a fit when she didn't bring our coats to us when we were leaving."

"You had to see yourselves out?" Tommy laughed. "I can't imagine my aunt was happy about that."

"She most certainly was not," Evelyn agreed. "She let it be known all the way back to the house that, in her day, housemaids simply would not have dared to act in such a manner."

"Poor Aunt Em," Tommy said. "I rather think the changes in the world since the war have come as a great shock to her."

"She would much rather things were as they used to be." Evelyn pointed at a cottage with a perfectly manicured hedge which afforded the home a little privacy from the prying eyes of the villagers as they walked down the lane. "It is this one."

Tommy opened the gate and took care to close it after they entered. He knocked on the door and stood back off the front step. "I hope they are not too afraid of the goings on that they dare not answer the door."

"Elsie seems a very sensible girl," Evelyn replied, just as the door opened.

"Lord Northmoor!" A woman exclaimed, pushing the door wider. She gasped. "And Lady Northmoor!"

"Mrs Warren?" Tommy enquired, wishing their presence didn't make the villagers act as though they were in the presence of royalty. It made him feel incredibly uncomfortable.

The woman pulled back her shoulders. "I am she."

"Would we be able to speak with Elsie, please?"

"Elsie?" Mrs Warren squeaked. "My Elsie is a good girl. She cannot possibly be mixed up in this terrible business."

"Actually," Tommy said, trying to use his smoothest and most persuasive voice. "We think Elsie may have seen something. We would like to talk to her as a possible witness. There is absolutely no suggestion that she has done anything wrong."

Of course, that wasn't entirely true. They definitely thought she had done something she shouldn't, but that thing was not murder.

Mrs Warren's shoulders sagged in relief. "You had better come in. I don't know what I am thinking leaving you both standing outside, especially on a day like this. It is bitterly cold."

Elsie's mother led them into a narrow hallway. A voice came from the back of the house, where Tommy presumed the kitchen was located.

"Who is it, Mother?"

Mrs Warren paused, then pushed open the door to the left of the corridor. "Please sit in the parlour and I will get Elsie."

Evelyn gestured towards their wellington boots and coats. "Should we take them off?"

Tommy peered into the small, but tidy room. "The fire isn't lit, we should probably keep them on."

"I think we should take off our boots…"

"Sssh!" Tommy raised a finger to his lips.

Frantic whispering could be heard coming from direction of the kitchen. Evelyn lent forward and pulled off her wet boots. "What do you think they are saying?"

"I mentioned Elsie seeing something. Perhaps her mother is asking what she could have seen sitting on the stool in front of the organ."

"Oh dear," Evelyn said quietly. "She may not tell us a thing if we have already got her into trouble with her mother."

"She's a grown woman," Tommy whispered back.

"She's an *unmarried* woman." Evelyn shook her head. "Living in a small village where reputation is everything. You men know nothing."

Tommy pulled off his own footwear as Mrs Warren reappeared, followed by a very reluctant looking Elsie.

"Lord Northmoor!" Mrs Warren said in an overly loud voice. "You really didn't need to take off your boots."

The woman's cheeks were pink and it wasn't difficult to work out that she was hopelessly embarrassed at receiving unexpected visitors that she had no idea what to do with.

"We couldn't possibly sit in your best room whilst wearing our outer garments." Evelyn moved into the room, but did not remove her coat.

Tommy followed and joined his wife on an overstuffed green patterned two-seater sofa. Mrs Warren hovered near the door. "Thank you so much, Mrs Warren."

For a moment, Tommy thought the woman was not going to take his not so subtle hint and leave them alone with Elsie. Slowly, however, she eventually backed out of the room.

"Should I make tea?" she asked nervously.

"That is very kind of you," Evelyn said. "But I fear I've had enough tea for one day."

Mrs Warren bobbed her head and closed the door behind her.

"Now, Elsie." Tommy leaned forward and rested his elbows on his knees. "We are not here to cause any trouble for you, but there are a few questions we would like you to answer."

"Trouble?" Elsie repeated weakly.

"A man is dead," Tommy said sternly. "Now is not the time for us to worry ourselves about what you were doing outside the church this morning."

"I.."

Tommy held up his hand. "You were seen coming back into the church. I do not wish to know what you were doing, or with whom. What I would like to know is if you saw anyone else outside?"

Elsie covered her face with her hands. "I am so ashamed. Oh, Lord Northmoor, my parents would be simply *mortified* if they knew I was with a married man."

"You were with Phillip Newley?"

Elsie shook her head in confusion. "No, I was with Leonard."

"Leonard Williams?" Evelyn asked.

The young woman dropped her hands to reveal bright red cheeks. "Please, you must not tell anyone."

"How long has this been going on?"

Evelyn nudged him sharply with her elbow. "I don't think that is relevant."

"Oh, My Lady. I know that it is wrong, but we love each other."

"Mr Williams is married with young children." Tommy shook his head. "This relationship reflects very badly on his character, and your own."

"He cannot have been involved in the murder," Elsie said as tears began falling down her cheeks.

"How can you be so sure?"

"He left the church and I followed only moments later."

"And you returned at the same time?"

Elsie shook her head and cried harder. "I came back in first. I don't know when Len returned. But it couldn't have been him."

"He was outside where the murder occurred." Tommy made an effort to calm his voice. He was aware from Evelyn's severe nudge that she thought he was being too stern with Elsie. However, he was hoping the authority in his tone frightened Elsie so much she told them the full truth.

The girl pulled a handkerchief out of her sleeve and dried her eyes. Eventually, she lifted her chin to face them. "We were not completely outside."

"Then please tell us where, exactly, you were." Tommy was quickly running out of patience with the simpering young woman.

"We were in the vestibule. When you enter the church, there's a little alcove with an old boot scraper. It allows us to hear what is happening in church, but not to be seen."

"Why would you put your hat on?" Evelyn asked. "That makes no sense to me whatsoever."

Elsie blew her nose. "It was on my knee. I just took it with me. I didn't think."

"And then you put it on your head because you didn't want to put it on the dirty floor?"

"Exactly that, My Lady."

Tommy got to his feet. "Thank you for being so honest. I do hope this incident will cause you to think twice about what you are doing. I say this only because you are a young girl who may well have been led astray by an older man who should know better."

"You won't tell?"

"If you have told us the absolute truth, we will have no need to speak of this to anyone else."

"Oh, thank you, My Lord. I have told you everything, I promise."

"Very well." Tommy nodded.

When they got outside, Tommy waited for the tirade that would surely come from Evelyn at his high-handedness. They had walked down the small path, and he had clicked the gate shut behind them before she spoke. "It was very fortunate your 'lord of the manor' act worked."

"Act?" he put his head on one side.

"She was terrified of you."

"If she was scared enough she told me nothing but the truth, then acting up to my title was worth it."

Evelyn pursed her lips. "I don't much like that side of you."

He couldn't think of a single thing to say in response because he didn't much like it either.

***

Evelyn couldn't remember a time she was so annoyed with Tommy. Usually he was the nicest, most placid man to walk the earth. Today he hadn't cajoled information from Elsie, as was his usual tactic, he had bullied it out of her.

"Are you angry with me because I went back to the manor without telling you?" she asked as they walked towards the vicarage.

Tommy sighed. "Not angry, no."

"Cross?"

He reached out an arm to stop her. "Upset, actually, if you want to know."

Evelyn gasped. "I upset you? Why?"

"We usually do this sleuthing business together." He looked earnestly at her. "I looked around for you, and you weren't there. When I saw the carriage was gone, I knew you had left without me."

"I knew you wouldn't leave the village until the murderer was caught."

"And I thought you wouldn't leave the village without me."

Evelyn lay a hand on his arm. "I won't always do what you think I should. You ought to know that about me by now. I was keen to get home and check on Nancy."

"But you came back."

"I returned because I feared Elsie may be in danger if the murderer thought she had seen something."

He looked away. "I hoped you might have missed me a little, and that is why you came back."

"I am quite used to taking care of myself, I do not always need to be with you," she snapped before she could stop herself. "I have had many years of practice, in case you might have forgot."

Two bright red spots of anger bloomed in Tommy's cheeks. "I see."

Evelyn bit her lip, she had gone too far. She had known it before the words left her mouth. They were the cruellest thing she could have said to him—it was not his fault they had spent years apart.

Ever chivalrous, he did not march off like many men would have done. Instead, he stood tall and straight and offered her his arm. She linked hers through and wanted nothing more than to lay her head on his shoulder and pretend their silly quarrel hadn't happened.

It took them only a couple of minutes to walk the short distance between Elsie Warren's house and the vicarage. Tommy raised the knocker and rapped smartly on the door.

Evelyn was afraid she might look like one of the icicles hanging from John's roof if she stood there much longer. After what felt like an interminable wait, the door was finally answered.

"You're back," Hilda said with no preamble, and not a trace of warmth.

"We would like to see the vicar, please," Tommy said. "And I do hope you won't mind if we trouble you for a hot drink, my wife is freezing."

Hilda opened the door wide enough for them to walk in but did not respond. Outside the door to the parlour, she knocked sharply on the door, and walked in without waiting for the vicar to respond.

"Lord and Lady Northmoor," she said dourly.

"Wonderful!" John said brightly. "Might we have tea?"

Evelyn hated how hopeful he sounded. As though the simple request might not be met with an easy acquiescence. "Do not trouble yourself on my account."

"Lord Northmoor?"

Tommy looked at Evelyn with a sad look on his face. "I…no, thank you."

Hilda shrugged, tutted and said tartly. "Please yourself."

As soon as they were seated, John held up a hand. "Don't say it."

Evelyn choked back a laugh, but it really was not amusing. The way Hilda spoke to John was not only impertinent but horribly disrespectful. "You must talk to her."

"I've tried." John grimaced. "It usually ends with me apologising."

"Perhaps I shall ask Aunt Em to pop into the kitchen next time she is in the village. I am sure she would soon put Hilda right."

John laughed. "I rather think she would vacate her post with immediate effect."

Evelyn tilted her head. "Would that be such a bad thing?"

The vicar pretended to consider that idea for a moment. "I suppose that wouldn't be the worst outcome. When do you think Lady Emily will have time?"

"You just say the word."

John laughed, then shook his head. "I should not be so uncharitable. She does her best."

Evelyn snorted. "She does nothing of the sort. I wonder if you might ask Elsie Warren to come back if Hilda does move on?"

"She was a very happy young thing." John smiled fondly. "And very eager to please. Polite to my guests, everything an old chap like me wants really."

"We've come about Elsie, in a roundabout way," Tommy said.

"Have you really? Whatever for?"

"We have promised not to divulge exactly what we spoke to Elsie about." Evelyn flashed Tommy a warning look.

"Don't worry, dear, I'm not about to let the cat out of the bag," Tommy replied stiffly.

She wasn't the only one surprised at how awkward his endearment sounded. John looked between them with one quizzical white brow raised.

"That sounds intriguing." He smiled at them both. "But I shall ask no more. Tell me what you are able, and I will help if I can."

"Elsie left the service part way through," Evelyn explained. "And we were worried she may have seen either the murderer or some clue as to who it may be."

"She left? Whatever for?" Evelyn waited until John gave a small nod. "I see. How very awkward."

"Did you find her an honest girl when she worked for you?"

"Incredibly so. As I said, I was very pleased with her work."

"And, as far as you know, there was no excessive attention shown by her towards gentlemen?"

"Not at all. She seemed a very good girl. Nothing like that at all. What a shame for her to now be mixed up in something unsavoury."

"I would hope that after we have spoken to her, she will rethink her relationship with the man in question."

"I shouldn't think she would dare so much as even look at him ever again after the way you spoke to her," Evelyn said tartly.

John's eyebrows shot up again. "Perhaps I shall have a brandy. It's been a difficult day and I rather think my nerves are on edge. Tommy, Evelyn, will you join me?"

Evelyn breathed in deeply and forced herself to relax. What was wrong with her? Why did she keep sniping at Tommy? "Not for me, thank you."

"Can I offer you something lighter? A gin perhaps? Maybe a nice sweet sherry?"

Evelyn shook her head. "Aunt Em and I had two gins before lunch had even been served. I am quite content."

John looked at Tommy. "Absolutely, I think a brandy would go down jolly well."

The vicar got to his feet and moved over to the small drinks trolley in the corner of his parlour. "Have you two identified the suspects?"

Tommy sighed. "It could almost be anyone in the entire village."

"But surely with your super sleuthing you have whittled down those most under suspicion?" John carried Tommy's drink to him, then returned to collect his own. "I have faith in the both of you, even if you do not have it in yourselves. Even this old man can see the uncertainty in your expressions."

"I know this might sound silly," Evelyn hesitated. "The previous murders we helped to solve did involve people we knew, but somehow this one feels more personal. Which makes no sense because we didn't like Phillip one little bit."

"We weren't very keen on Uncle Charles either," Tommy admitted. "But Evelyn is right, this has a very personal feel about it and I am quite unnerved."

"Perhaps it is because we lived in the village," Evelyn mused. "The suspects are not just people we know, they are our friends, people who regularly served us in village shops."

"That would explain why you are both feeling so out of sorts." John sipped his brandy. "It has rather stopped me worrying quite so much about the missing money from the collection plate."

"I believe you suspected Phillip Newley of taking that?"

"I had no proof whatsoever," John admitted. "My only reason for thinking it was him was simply because I knew of his character."

"And if he were not in the village, where would your suspicions fall then?" Tommy asked.

John did not hesitate. "The wardens are the ones who take care of the plates when the collection has been made. They would be the most likely suspects."

"Alfred Cross and Leonard Williams?" Evelyn confirmed.

"I cannot imagine either of them doing something dishonest." John shook his head sadly. "But I know someone did. Percy Armstrong was adamant he put a ten shilling note in the plate each week for some months now. He was most put out when he discovered at the committee meeting our funds did not seem to support his donations."

"Given we all agree Phillip Newley was a thoroughly bad fellow, is it possible he had something on Len or Alf and he was forcing them to steal on his behalf?" Tommy wondered.

"He seemed to have plenty of money to have a good drink every Saturday night for a man just out of prison," Evelyn added.

John finished his brandy and placed the tumbler on the table next to him. "Blackmail is such a dishonourable crime."

"I couldn't agree more, vicar," Tommy said. "Though I don't think there was much honour shown in the way Mr Newley was dispatched from this earth."

Chapter Six

"Truce?" Tommy suggested as they left the vicarage.

"We work much better together than separately," Evelyn agreed.

She put out her hand to shake Tommy's but he lifted it to his lips, nudged her glove out of the way and kissed the inside of her wrist. "Len's next?"

Evelyn nodded in agreement. "We should divide and conquer when we get there."

"How so?"

"I shall get his wife out of the way, and you must quiz Len about the money and Elsie."

Tommy frowned. "I still don't see how Len would have been able to slip out undiscovered and kill Phillip if he was with Elsie."

"We can never see the full story at this stage of an investigation." Evelyn reminded him. "Usually everything is a huge muddle and nothing at all makes sense."

"And, of course, we also must remember that not everyone tells us the truth. Or, at least, they may tell us *part* of the truth, but not everything that we need to know to put all the pieces together."

They walked down the path, past the pub, the butcher's and Percy Armstrong's establishment before they came to a small lane that led to Leonard and Dorothy Williams' modest home.

The cottage belonging to Elsie Warren had clearly been well kept. The same could not be said for that of the church warden. The guttering to the left of the front door hung at a precarious angle and the hedge along the path was so overgrown they had to push it out of the way to get to the gate.

"Do you think the vicar would think it uncharitable of me to suggest that Len spends too much time on other pursuits and not enough on maintaining his home life?" Tommy asked grimly.

"Absolutely." Evelyn nodded. "He would think it very mean-spirited, yet I think it is very accurate. The entire place has a very unloved look about it."

Tommy knocked on the door and stamped his feet. "The weather is turning again. I expect we shall have more snow before long."

A woman's voice shouted something unintelligible before the door was yanked abruptly open. "Yes?"

Her expression changed as she realised who had come calling. Mrs Williams had a rather round, ruddy face and wore a stained apron over a plain brown dress. Elsie Warren was everything this woman was not—youthful, vibrant, and self assured.

"We are very sorry to interrupt your afternoon, Mrs Williams. We wondered if we might have a few moments of your husband's time?"

"Len?" Mrs Williams gulped. "What would you be wanting with my Len?"

"He sits at the back of the church," Tommy explained. "We are wondering if he saw anything."

"We're good God fearing folk," Mrs Williams said, but she sounded to Tommy like she was trying to convince herself rather than him. "We keep ourselves to ourselves."

"Perhaps if we could have a very quick word, if it's not too much trouble?"

Reluctantly, Dorothy Williams opened the door wide enough to allow them to enter. The hallway was littered with discarded boots, muddy footprints trailed to the back of the house where a cacophony of noise suggested several rowdy children.

"How many children do you have, Mrs Williams?" Evelyn asked in her most polite voice. "I should love to meet them."

"Why on earth would you be wanting to do that?" Mrs Williams looked at her in disbelief.

"I like children very much."

"Do you?" she responded doubtfully. "You don't have any of your own, do you?"

Evelyn smiled brightly but Tommy felt a stab of pain he was sure rivalled that of his wife's. "We have not yet been blessed."

"Lead the way, Mrs Williams." Tommy encouraged. "Lady Northmoor is obviously keen to enjoy the company of your children whilst I speak with your husband. Where might I find him?"

"He's in there." Dorothy jerked a thumb towards the parlour, with a long suffering sniff of discontentment. "Reading the newspaper."

"How many children do you have?" Tommy heard Evelyn's question as the stout woman led the way to the kitchen at the back of the house.

He just caught the answer before he knocked gently on the parlour door. "Six, and they wear me out, I don't mind telling you."

"I've told you, woman, don't disturb me while I'm reading my paper." The response was loud and clear through the firmly closed door.

Tommy called back. "Awfully sorry to disturb your Sunday, Mr Williams, but it's Lord Northmoor."

There was a vague sound of rustling before a chair creaked and the door opened. A fire roared in the hearth, a pair of comfortable slippers rested in front of an old armchair.

"Sorry, My Lord, thought it was the wife. She knows this is my one day off a week, but she can't keep those kids under control. I can barely concentrate on reading my paper for the noise."

Tommy nodded, temporarily lost for words. He hadn't really considered Leonard Williams before, but he did now. The other man was of medium height and build. His mid brown hair was thinning on top and held in place over his scalp with an over abundance of pomade. What on earth did a pretty young girl like Elsie Warren see in such a man? Tommy was yet to see any redeeming qualities that could have attracted her.

"I have a few questions for you, if you don't mind?"

"About that fellow's murder, I suppose?"

Well it wasn't to be about the price of cheese, was it?

Tommy choked back the sarcastic response and quickly schooled his features into a blank mask. It wouldn't do at all to get the man's back up before he had even asked a single question. "That's right, terrible business."

"What's it got to do with me?"

"Are you aware that money has gone missing from the collection plate?"

Len's face immediately turned belligerent. "And because I don't live in a big, posh house you immediately think it was me?"

"Actually, no." Tommy inched his way forward, wanting to be inside the stuffy parlour before he asked Len about his relationship with Elsie. "Perhaps this would be better if we sat down and talked man to man."

Len stared at him for a long moment before finally acquiescing, closing the parlour door, and sitting in the chair next to the fire. He immediately lifted his feet to rest on the fender. The crumpled newspaper at his feet suggested to Tommy that the other man had been enjoying an afternoon snooze while his wife battled to keep the children out of mischief.

Tommy stood to the side and shuffled his booted feet awkwardly. When it was quite apparent Len was not going to offer him a seat, he decided to get his quest over and done with as quickly as possible.

"It is my understanding that you have been having a relationship with Miss Elsie Warren."

"Why, you bloody upstart! You can't come into my home and ask me such impertinent questions. Who do you think you are?"

"The police have given me permission to look into the matter involving the death of Phillip Newley until they are able to get through to the village."

It wasn't quite the actual truth, but it was close enough.

"And how does that one thing have anything to do with the other thing you just asked?"

"I am not sure," Tommy answered honestly. "However, Miss Warren was seen slipping back into the church at about the time of the murder so we were obliged to question her."

"I still don't see what that has to do with me," Len replied obstinately.

"Miss Warren gave you as her alibi."

"She said she was with me?" Len asked furiously. "The lying little cat."

"That's most unfortunate." Tommy shook his head in mock sadness. "If you were not with Miss Warren, that means she has no alibi for the time of the murder."

"She probably had a lover's tiff with that fellow and killed him."

"Mr Williams," Tommy said slowly and clearly. "That leaves you in a very tenuous position, I am afraid."

"What are you talking about, man?"

"If you were not with Miss Warren, where were you?"

"I was in the church."

"I do not wish to call you a liar, Mr Williams." Tommy looked directly at the other man. "But you were not. When Mr Cross had his funny turn, you were nowhere to be seen."

Len opened his mouth, closed it again, and glared at Tommy furiously. "I…"

"Might you want to rethink the alibi Miss Warren offered?"

"She is a loose woman." Len put his head in his hands, but Tommy was not fooled by his sudden display of shame. The man was simply dismayed that he had been caught out. "She parades around in those shameful high heels and sheer stockings. I have resisted her for months. This morning, I am humiliated to admit that I allowed myself to be led to a little alcove off the entrance to the church and kissed her."

"Thank you for clearing that up." Tommy swallowed down the nasty taste in his mouth left by Len's pathetic play acting. "And to clarify, you know nothing about the missing money? Phillip Newley was not aware of a dalliance for which he may have been blackmailing you?"

Hate filled Len's eyes. "I have just told you. There was no 'dalliance'. I was tempted after months of provocation. I know nothing about the missing money. I would like you to leave now."

"I would be most happy to oblige you, Mr Williams." Tommy marched to the door and called along the corridor to Evelyn.

He let himself out, content to wait on the doorstep until Evelyn was ready to leave. Len Williams had got under his skin. It had been a long time since Tommy had wanted to punch someone on the nose quite as badly as he wanted to right at that moment.

***

"He's a quite despicable man," Tommy raged as they walked back down the lane towards the pub. "He was content to hang Elsie out to dry until he realised that left him without an alibi. And he completely blamed her for what has been going on."

"Despicable," Evelyn echoed. She had long since learned that when Tommy was on a tirade, there was little point in interrupting him because he would not hear or comprehend anything she had to say.

"I was quite furious with Elsie, but now I feel jolly sorry for her. What do you think possessed her to fall in love with such an odious man?"

Content it was now safe to speak, Evelyn didn't hesitate. "I don't think one chooses who to fall in love with."

"There's a village full of nice fellows." Tommy shrugged. "*Single* fellows."

"You live in the past too much," Evelyn said morosely. "What nice young, single men are there in the village?"

"Well, there are some."

"Name me one."

Tommy turned to look at her. "Goodness, you're right. How awful."

"So you see, poor Elsie was bound to fall in love with whoever paid her the slightest bit of attention."

"She's such a bright, pretty young thing though," Tommy said mournfully. "She deserves so much better."

"Village life is changing, much like the rest of the world."

"Is that realisation what has made you so unsettled?"

Evelyn pondered his question. "Unsettled is a very good question. That is precisely how I feel."

Tommy thoughtfully changed the subject. "I think we should speak to Annie next, do you?"

"Yes, let us speak to her about where she believed George to be this morning. He usually attends morning worship doesn't he?"

"He does indeed. Let us hope that she can shed some light on his whereabouts. I should hate for us not to be able to clear him before the police arrive. He is sure to be the person they focus their interests on."

Evelyn hunched her shoulders against the cold. "I feel so desperately sorry for him. However, I must tell you that his demeanour when he came into the church was more than a little frightening."

"How so?"

"His eyes were a little wild looking and he didn't seem to know where he was."

"Is it possible he could have been sleepwalking?"

"I suppose *anything* is possible. I don't have knowledge of such things but perhaps either Teddy or Reg would be able to give us some guidance."

"Let's learn what we can from Annie and then we will pull together what we know.

"We don't really know what's happening though, do we? What do we have to tell them?"

Tommy looked Evelyn. "We have precisely nothing to tell them. However, I don't think we can let them go to their beds tonight without reassuring them that we are doing our very best to solve this murder. They need to know that we are working diligently to conclude this matter before the police arrive. If nothing else, it may help them to sleep more soundly."

"Your optimism is commendable."

"You don't have any?"

"I don't seem to have as much as you do."

They reached the front door of the pub. Tommy pushed it open and found Partridge fast asleep in one of the chairs in front of the fire, an empty plate in front of him. "It looks as though Partridge has found Mrs O'Connell's hamper."

"I do hope he has left a little for us, I don't want to impose on Mrs Hughes' hospitality any more than we need to. Not when Mr Hughes is so clearly unwell."

"I'll go up and see if Mrs Hughes has time to talk with us now. I should also ensure she is happy for us both to stay here tonight."

The upstairs sleeping quarters for the Hughes family, and their paying guests, were accessed by a door behind the bar. No sooner had Tommy gone through the door than the front door crashed open.

Evelyn startled and stepped backwards, towards the sleeping Partridge. One hand flew up to cover her mouth. Too surprised to even murmur her fear, let alone scream out loud she stood trembling.

"Behind me, My Lady!" Partridge moved quickly for a man who had, only moments before, been sleeping soundly.

He roughly pushed her towards the chair he had occupied and moved towards the entrance of the pub. Two distinct thumps sounded followed by quick, muffled footsteps. It sounded as though someone had discarded their boots and was walking towards them in stockinged feet.

"Good afternoon, Lady Northmoor," Teddy greeted her warmly. "I understand I've missed a good deal of activity whilst I've been busy with the sick and injured."

"Teddy, I'm very glad to see you. And in one piece I might add!" Evelyn turned to Partridge. "Thank you for so diligently racing to my rescue."

Partridge nodded and returned to his seat looking flustered at being caught asleep by his mistress.

Dr Theodore Mainwaring grimaced. "I understand the same cannot be said for poor Phillip Newley."

Evelyn couldn't bring herself to utter the standard phrase 'sadly not'. She wasn't particularly unhappy he was no longer about, but the manner of his death was certainly to be regretted.

"You've heard then?"

"Isolde told me," he admitted. "She also said there was some concern about where I have been this morning."

"It certainly would have been better if we had known where you were." Evelyn bit her lip. "Is Isolde very cross with me?"

"I explained to her the responsibility you and Tommy feel for the village. I think she understands now that neither of you will settle until you know the villagers are safe." Teddy unwound a red scarf from around his neck and draped it and his coat on the back of one of the chairs. "I'm positively famished."

"Mrs O'Connell sent a fully stocked hamper," Evelyn said. "It's in the kitchen, help yourself. Partridge already has."

"My Lady…"

Evelyn held up a hand. "I was pulling your leg. No one minds that you helped yourself. The food is for anyone who has a need. Cook did not mean it for Tommy alone, she has packed enough to last several people for days."

Tommy came back through the dark oak door marked 'private' with Mrs Hughes who looked as though she had spent every minute since her husband was discovered in such an agitated state crying her eyes out.

"Jolly glad to see you." Tommy greeted Teddy and clapped him on the back. "Absolutely perfect timing. I have some things to ask Mrs Hughes and you may be able to give us your professional opinion on a few things."

"I'm always happy to assist in any way I can." Teddy spread his arms wide and pulled out a seat for Mrs Hughes.

"Now, Mrs Hughes," Tommy began.

"Please call me Annie, My Lord." She rubbed her hands together. "I'm quite nervous enough talking to you without you using my full name. Everyone just calls me Annie."

"Very well." Tommy inclined his head. "I would like to know if you can tell me where George was this morning. Specifically, did he walk to church with you?"

"He did not." Annie looked nervously up at the ceiling as though her husband could hear every word. "I thought he had left before me. Last time I saw him, he was heading outside to clear the path in front of the pub and along the lane a little way."

"What time would that have been?"

"I would guess around half past nine. We generally leave at nine forty five as a rule."

"And you didn't see him again until you returned to the church with the pint you had pulled for Alfred Cross?"

"That is correct." Annie leaned forward slightly. "Though honestly, My Lord, the pint was an excuse to get out of church and look for George."

"Were you worried about him?"

Annie looked over at Evelyn. "He has these spells where he shakes and doesn't seem to know where he is. You saw that last year, My Lady."

"I did." Evelyn nodded. "He was most distressed."

"That was when the unfortunate Mr Franklin was discovered?"

"Is it a disturbing event such as the sight of blood that causes Mr Hughes to be distressed?"

"If only." Annie shook her head, anger forming tight lines around her mouth. "If only there were specific situations that caused him to be upset. If he didn't have the nightmares so often then…"

She snapped her mouth firmly closed.

"Then?" Tommy asked gently. "What else, Mrs Hughes?"

"I can't say." She closed her eyes.

"Do you trust me to do the right thing?"

"I trust you, My Lord."

"And the doctor, and my wife?"

Slowly Annie Hughes nodded her head. "I suppose none of you can do him any harm, and the one that has is gone. Can't say as I'm upset at that."

"Phillip Newley has caused you harm?" Tommy asked sharply.

"He threatened to cause us great personal harm," Mrs Hughes corrected.

"In what way?"

"He said he would make it known that my George was a raving lunatic and people wouldn't want to stay here anymore." Annie rubbed a hand over her eyes.

"And he thought his word would put people off from staying at your establishment?"

"He told us he knew people who would spread the word of George's lunacy." Annie pulled a face. "And then he told us that if we let him stay with us for free, he would keep his mouth shut."

"That certainly explains how he has been able to stay in the village for so long without a job."

"He always has money for a pint," Annie said bitterly. "So he was clearly running some other swindle too. It's no wonder someone decided enough was enough and bumped him off."

"Indeed. Thank you, Mrs Hughes."

Tommy looked over at Evelyn and she gave him a small nod. There was nothing else they should ask the unfortunate woman at this time.

Chapter Seven

"I suppose it is my turn to be interrogated," Teddy said wryly when Mrs Hughes had gone back upstairs to sit with her husband.

"I prefer to think of it as a friendly little chat, old man," Tommy replied. "But first, I'd like to ask you about George Hughes, if I may?"

"His nightmares and the reason why he experiences episodes where he gets distressed and confused?"

"If you are able to help me understand those things, it would definitely help."

"It's not my area of expertise but an eminent psychologist has suggested it is something known as 'shellshock'. A large percentage of people with shellshock also have what is medically known as neurasthenia."

Tommy looked down at his leg, remembering his now healed injury. He had never doubted he escaped the ravages of the war relatively easily, unlike many men he served with. "What is that?"

"It's a term that covers lots of different ailments. Basically, it is a weakness of the nerves and sufferers have symptoms such as fatigue, anxiety, and a depressed mood."

"I don't suppose you are able to share whether George has this condition?"

Teddy shook his head. "You know that, as his doctor, I am not at liberty to divulge that kind of information."

"Poor George, what a terrible burden for him to bear." Evelyn reached under the table and put her hand on top of Tommy's.

"I didn't say…" Teddy began.

"You have said enough." Tommy looked at Evelyn and the two exchanged a tender look. "We have read the newspapers. We understand a little of how many people still believe these poor fellows need to just get a hold of themselves, as though they are lacking in moral fibre somehow."

"It is shocking that more has not been done for them," Teddy agreed.

"I wish it were possible for there to be a William Christie House in every city in the entire country. George is lucky he has his wife to care for him. My heart aches for those who are not so lucky." Evelyn squeezed Tommy's hand as she referred to the large building that Tommy had converted in York for soldiers who were down on their luck.

"Let us turn to the murder." Tommy smiled at Evelyn. "I feel so very helpless thinking of all the men I would like to help. From what you have told us, is it possible that George, should he be suffering from shellshock or neurasthenia, could have committed the murder and be completely unaware of having done so?"

"It is possible." Teddy stroked his thick moustache, as was his habit when he was pondering a question. "Though, if those were his issues, I would have thought it more likely the crime would've been committed with George's bare hands, or perhaps his old service revolver."

76

"As though he believed he was killing the enemy?"

"Exactly that." Teddy smoothed down his whiskers. "A knife feels wrong to me. It suggests a pre-arranged meeting and therefore premeditation. Of course, these are simply my thoughts, I am not a psychologist."

"We must make finding out if anyone has a knife missing a priority," Tommy said. "And perhaps we should take steps to try…"

He stopped talking as Evelyn pinched the skin on the back of his hand. He was about to ask her what she was doing until he realised his error. They did not know who the murderer was, and they shouldn't discuss the murder and their plans for solving it in front of someone who must remain a suspect.

"I'm very sorry to ask, Teddy," Evelyn said. "But we really must ask you to account for your movements this morning."

"Do you have a specific time frame in mind?"

Tommy couldn't help but realise his friend had not immediately declared his innocence. Usually a person who wasn't involved would do that first. Teddy was a clever man. If he was guilty of this crime, he would've taken the time to give himself an unshakeable alibi and cover up any traces of his involvement.

"It stopped snowing at around eight this morning. The marks left in the snow from footprints suggest they were left around the time the snow stopped falling. Or, at least, not long before otherwise they would have started to fill back up with snow."

"Hmm." Teddy drummed his fingers on the table. "So I suppose you are asking where I was from around six this morning, when it was snowing heavily, until the body was discovered?"

"Yes." Tommy frowned. The timeline was correct, he was quite sure of that. The problem was how someone could have persuaded Phillip Newley to meet with them in the churchyard. Surely there were more accessible areas to meet in and around the village?

"I was awake before six," Teddy said, resting his chin on his hands as though reliving his movements that day. "I remember looking outside and seeing how much snow had fallen overnight. My first call of the day came not long after I had finished breakfast. You will understand I cannot give names of my patients?"

Tommy grinned. "I understand that you cannot, but that village gossip being what it is, finding out will be jolly easy."

"That is true." Teddy smiled in return. "That call was to a farmer who had slipped outside his cowshed and cut his arm on a nail sticking out of the barn door. I returned home, and reassured Mrs Hamilton that little Bertie having a bump on his head from the kitchen table was not going to permanently addle his brains. Next I visited a lady who was concerned about her unborn child. Thereafter I went to another farm where the farmer's wife had fallen on her garden path and twisted her ankle."

"Mrs Hamilton is a very concerned parent, is she not?"

"I should not discuss my patients," Teddy reminded Tommy. "But I will say that if I were to get paid for every visit I made to that house I would be very rich indeed."

"You didn't see anything unusual as you moved around the village?"

Teddy choked back a sound of amusement. "Like a knife wielding lunatic or someone covered in blood?"

Tommy pressed his lips together in a firm line of displeasure. "I mean anything at all abnormal. Even something very small could matter hugely."

"Sorry." Teddy dropped his head in consternation. "That was in poor taste. I saw nothing."

"We should go see Isolde," Evelyn suggested. "We need to find out when she last saw Phillip."

Teddy stood, wrapped his scarf around his neck and picked up his coat. "I'll walk with you."

***

Teddy walked with them to the path leading to Isolde's cottage. As soon as he had continued on the path to his own home and was out of earshot, Evelyn turned to Tommy. "You told Teddy we will be trying to find out if anyone has a knife missing from their kitchen. If he killed Phillip, he now has plenty of time to get rid of the weapon."

"If Teddy is our killer, he will have already divested himself of the murder weapon." Tommy grimaced. "But I take your point, it was a foolish thing for me to say."

"It's not like you to be so careless." Evelyn patted his arm, deciding she had said enough. His face when Teddy had spoken about George had been utterly full of pain and it had made Evelyn regret her earlier sharpness with Tommy even more.

It wasn't his fault, any more than it was her own, that pregnancy hadn't immediately occurred the very moment she decided it was what she wanted. By nature she wasn't a selfish woman, but that was precisely how she had been acting. She would do well to remember the broken shell of a man that the army had sent home to her and be thankful that Tommy had recovered as well as he had. Other men, like George, had not been so fortunate.

The night had started drawing in and although Tommy had suggested earlier the snow was going to start once more, it had not. However, it was dark and getting colder by the minute.

"Should we make this our last call for the evening?"

"I think that is best," Tommy agreed. "Annie has a room made up for us. She has also given us permission to search Phillip's room."

"Given what we have found out, and suspect about that man, his room could be an absolute treasure trove of clues. We should perhaps have checked there first."

Tommy patted her hand. "It is so difficult to decide what to prioritise when there is only the two of us. Ordinarily we may be able to trust our friends to help us, but in this case our friends could turn out to be the very people who are the most untrustworthy."

He opened the garden gate and Evelyn preceded Tommy down the garden path. Abruptly, she stopped walking, and pointed at the small patch of lawn hidden beneath its blanket of snow. "Do you see that?"

"It looks like footprints."

"That's what I thought." Evelyn turned to look at Tommy. "And it appears that they go all of the way round to the back of the house."

"They don't look particularly fresh,"

"Why do you say that?"

"The edges are not crisp, as though a shoe or boot has just stepped in the snow." Tommy shrugged. "We probably shouldn't guess things we don't know, should we? That's just my impression. It wouldn't be wise of us to rely on things we suppose."

"I agree with your thoughts, they do look old, but we shouldn't speculate. Why would someone walk across the lawn and to the back of the house when the front door is right there?"

"Someone who wished not to be discovered standing on Isolde's doorstep waiting to be let in."

"You are thinking of Teddy. But, equally, it could be someone sneaking around for nefarious reasons." Evelyn stared at her husband. "Do you know something I don't? Has Teddy be making visits to Isolde that necessitate this level of subterfuge?"

Tommy spread his hands wide. "I don't know anything of the kind. However, you know what village gossip is."

"There isn't any about Teddy and Isolde. Nora explicity said so, and it seems that the butcher's wife knows everything there is to know." Evelyn looked thoughtfully at Tommy. "That does seem rather odd, doesn't it?"

"Hessleham seems to have quite accepted that they have an attraction for each other that cannot be explored because of Isolde's marriage."

"And yet…"

"I don't understand?" Tommy frowned.

"And yet her reaction to my suggestion that we cannot rule Teddy out of our investigations was very powerful."

"Ah." Tommy nodded. "And Teddy told us that Isolde told him of Phillip's death which means he visited her when he came back from visiting his last patient."

"I wonder if it is possible that they have a relationship they have successfully kept from everyone."

Tommy looked doubtful again. "That seems most improbable. The villagers know *everything*! Consider how much gossip Nora told you."

Evelyn marched the few steps up to the door and knocked loudly. Friends or not, she intended to get as much information out of Isolde as she could. In her peripheral vision, she noticed the pale flowered curtains to the right of the door twitched.

Despite Teddy's assurances that Isolde now understood the need for them to investigate each suspect thoroughly, the new widow did not look happy to see Tommy and Evelyn when she opened the door to them.

She did not sound pleased either. "I wondered how long it would be until you two showed up."

"Good afternoon, Isolde," Tommy said pleasantly.

"Lord Northmoor." She briefly nodded her head, but her lips did not spread into her usual ready smile.

"May we come in?" Evelyn did her best to sound as normal as possible, but her voice sounded stilted even to her ears.

Isolde gave a jaunty wave over Evelyn's shoulder. "You had better. You are attracting the attention of my neighbours."

She led them into her comfortable parlour. A chair sat on either side of the fire, which was lit but needed stoking and more coal added. Tommy leaned over and looked into the coal scuttle. "Shall I fill this for you?"

"I couldn't let you do that. I shall do it after you've left."

"It would be no trouble."

Evelyn knew exactly what Tommy was doing and hoped fervently that Isolde did not. He wanted an excuse to both check out the back garden and to give her some time alone with Isolde in the hope her friend would answer Evelyn's questions more easily.

"I can do it," Isolde said stiffly. "Please have a seat."

The chair on the right had a small table next to it. On the table stood a mug and an empty side plate. Evelyn chose the other chair. "Have we interrupted your supper?"

"I had a sandwich earlier." Tears shone in Isolde's eyes. "I haven't been very hungry since it all happened."

"Of course not," Evelyn consoled. "You poor darling. It's a perfectly dreadful thing to happen."

Isolde dabbed her eyes. "I feel an absolute fraud weeping over someone we are all aware I had no agreeable feelings towards."

Evelyn struggled for the right words. "At one time you must have loved him very much."

"I think I did. It's hard to remember any fond feelings I had for him. Especially because he has been so loathsome since turning up in Hessleham."

"In what way?" Tommy asked from his position standing behind Evelyn's chair.

"He badgered me most persistently." Isolde shuddered. "It didn't seem to matter where I was, or if I was talking to someone, he would approach me and remind me of our vows and insist his rightful place was at my side."

"And the other rumours?" Evelyn asked carefully.

"About the ten shilling note he tried to pass to Percy Armstrong you mean?"

"There is also money missing from the church collection plate," Tommy added.

Isolde wiped her eyes again. "John thinks that was Phillip?"

"He has no evidence whatsoever. Apparently the money started going missing around the same time Phillip arrived and, of course, John is aware of Phillip's background."

"Theft, fraud, but nothing that would give me grounds for divorce. I wished...no." Isolde shook her head. "I *prayed* that he would have an affair so I could start proceedings against him and put the whole sorry business of our marriage behind me."

"You were not aware of any signs he had committed adultery?"

"Sadly, no." Isolde put the crumbled handkerchief in her lap and played with the chain around her neck. "He seemed to find endless ways to embarrass me but never that...the one thing I wanted him to do."

"Isolde, please talk to me about that jewellery." Evelyn leaned forward and indicated the delicate necklace. "I know it's new and your reaction when I noticed it this morning makes me believe it has importance."

"It has importance to me," Isolde said stridently. "It was a present from Teddy."

Isolde pulled the necklace out from where it had been tucked underneath her blouse. A delicate diamond winked from a simple setting in what could only be described as an engagement ring.

"It's very beautiful."

"Yes, it is, isn't it?" Isolde agreed. "Teddy told me this afternoon I should show you because he is not ashamed of his love for me. That is why he bought me this ring. It is a symbol of his feelings for me. While we were aware that our feelings could never be spoken of, other than to each other, he wanted to give me a token of his affection."

Evelyn heard what Isolde did not say. They were all aware a relationship was not possible out in the open, but that did not mean their feelings had not been acted upon privately.

"I can see why you did not want to tell me that this morning."

"I was so afraid." Isolde picked up the handkerchief as her tears started flowing once more. "I am still so very frightened. Now you have seen that Teddy and I have not been content to remain only friends, as we led you to believe, suspicion falls even more heavily on him."

"That is true, it is pointless for me to pretend otherwise." Tommy tapped Evelyn's shoulder. "We should probably get back to the pub and let Isolde get on."

"You mustn't concentrate on Teddy alone!" Isolde cried. "Please do not let the way he feels about me blind you to other suspects."

"We would never do that." Evelyn embraced her friend quickly. "You know us well enough to be sure that we will do everything we can to identify the person who killed Phillip. We shall follow every lead. Rest assured that Teddy isn't the only person under suspicion."

Evelyn followed Tommy outside. They waited until they were walking down the deserted country lane before talking.

"I suppose you noticed the pair of man's slippers poking out from under the chair in which you were sitting?" Tommy asked.

"Hard to miss them." Evelyn sighed. "I had hoped that Isolde had learned from last time that being completely honest immediately is much easier than spouting half truths."

"I think Teddy knew it was snowing at six this morning because that is what time he left Isolde's home to return to his own."

"I fear that you are right."

"My biggest worry is that he arranged to meet Phillip early this morning to either ask him to leave the village or beg him to divorce Isolde. Or, perhaps, Teddy was going to try and pay him off."

Evelyn sighed. "I desperately hope it was someone else."

Even as she spoke, she accepted Teddy was the most obvious suspect and if the police were to

arrive in Hessleham in the morning they would
have no hesitation in arresting him immediately.

Chapter Eight

With deflated spirits, Tommy and Evelyn arrived back at the pub. Whilst Teddy encouraging Isolde to tell the truth about the ring he had given her was a good sign, there were too many other things hinting at further secrets.

Their good friend had the motive and the opportunity to have killed Phillip, and given the murder weapon was a sharp knife he certainly had the means.

"I'm quite worn out," Tommy said as he shrugged out of his coat. "It feels as though today has been never ending."

"I should have thought to pack us an overnight bag." Evelyn wrinkled her nose in distaste. "We shall have to wear the same clothes tomorrow."

"I would be happy to go back to the house and collect whatever you might need, My Lady." Partridge got to his feet.

"I forbid you to do such a thing," Evelyn responded. "I am very grateful for the offer, but it is my own lack of foresight that has put us into this position. I won't hear of you putting yourself out for me again today."

"As you wish, My Lady." Partridge took his seat once more.

"Mrs Hughes has kindly given us rooms for this evening, Partridge," Tommy told his estate manager. "I hope you will use the room and not insist on sitting in that chair all night."

"I will wake if anyone comes near the pub," Partridge responded. "But for safety's sake, you should probably lock your door, My Lord."

"Are you thinking of George?" Tommy whispered the question.

"He's a fabulous chap," Partridge answered. "When he is thinking straight. It was very sad to see him as he was this morning."

"You're quite right," Tommy agreed. "It is the prudent thing to do. I still don't feel happy about you sleeping down here."

"I've slept in much worse places, My Lord."

Tommy laughed. "I'm not sure I want to know."

"Shall I see about heating up some of the soup I know Mrs O'Connell put in the hamper? I'm famished. It seems so long ago since luncheon."

"If we were at the manor, it would still be hours before dinner." Tommy rubbed his stomach. "But some of Cook's soup and thick slices of bread and butter would be fabulous right now."

As Evelyn moved towards the pub kitchen, Mrs Hughes came bustling through the door. "George is awake, My Lord, I thought you would like to speak to him."

"Of course, Mrs Hughes, I shall come right up."

"Would George like some soup, Mrs Hughes?" Evelyn asked. "Cook has sent a hamper packed with food. Poor Partridge struggled to carry it inside."

"Oh, I couldn't let you fetch food for my George."

"Nonsense," Evelyn said briskly. "I shall bring a tray upstairs with food for both of you and leave it outside your room. Tommy can pass it through to you when you've finished speaking."

"My Lady, really…"

"She's very stubborn when she's made her mind up, Annie." Tommy put a hand under the woman's elbow. "It's useless arguing with her. Let us not keep George waiting."

Tommy sat in the chair Annie indicated next to George's bed. The other man was propped up and looked much better than he had the last time he had seen him.

"My Lord," George said as soon as Tommy was seated. "I am so embarrassed that you had to see me the way I was this morning."

"Nonsense," Tommy said briskly. "You tried your best to save a man's life and were then, understandably, upset that you had not been able to do so."

"You believe that I did not kill him?"

"If you tell me that you didn't, George, then I must believe that."

Tommy was once again struck by the thought that Teddy had not denied involvement. George, despite his obvious distress that morning had immediately been keen to ensure Tommy did not believe he could have committed the heinous crime.

"Did you find the weapon?" George asked, leaning forward and grabbing the cuff of Tommy's jacket. "You must find the weapon so no one else can be hurt."

"You're absolutely right, my good chap." Tommy was furious that he hadn't thought of that himself. It could be a crucial clue. "I wish I knew where to look."

George let out a mirthless laugh. "It won't be in the duck pond, My Lord, that's for certain."

Ordinarily it would be an excellent place to throw something a person never wanted found again. The duck pond was opposite the pub, next to the lane that led up to the manor house. Due to the inclement weather, it was completely frozen over. Of course, there were open fields behind the churchyard. The knife could have been thrown there.

"You should get that young dog of Lady Northmoor's down here," Annie said. "He soon sniffed out Mr Franklin's handkerchief that his crazy killer wiped their bloody hands on."

"That is a champion idea, Annie, thank you for suggesting it."

"She's got a good head on her shoulders." George smiled fondly at his wife.

"What did you think about Phillip Newley?"

"Not very much, to be honest, My Lord. He paid the bill for his room on time and never took liberties by asking for credit for his beer. Needless to say, he wasn't a nice chap, but he didn't cause us any trouble."

"Why do you say he wasn't a nice chap?"

"He could be rude to villagers. I heard he tried to swindle Percy out of money at his shop, and even though he supposedly wanted Mrs Newley to take him back he was always talking to other ladies."

"I have heard that from other people." Tommy wasn't surprised to hear that Annie had kept the worst of Phillip's behaviour from her husband. "He was a jolly handsome chap, so I expect ladies were taken in by his charm."

"Handsome is as handsome does," Annie muttered.

"My Annie wouldn't have her head turned by a man such as that. Would you, love?"

Annie moved round to the other side of the bed and kissed George's cheek. "Whyever would I want to look at another man when I have you?"

A discreet knock sounded at the door.

"Ah, that'll be Evelyn with your soup."

"Lady Northmoor has brought us soup?" George rubbed a hand over his jaw. "Goodness me. A lady such as that should not be waiting on the likes of us."

"We're staying in a room tonight and not being charged a penny," Tommy argued. "Evelyn is simply returning a favour."

"You're not charging them?" George winked at Annie. "They're landed gentry, my girl, you should be charging double."

Tommy laughed. "I can see you're feeling better. I shall leave you to get some of Mrs O'Connell's soup inside you. It comes with a guarantee of a restorative return to physical health."

George's smile slid from his face. "Wish she had some that would do the same with my head."

"Time is a great healer," Tommy said, then wished he could take back the trite words. They were not likely to give a man as proud as George Hughes any comfort. "Thank you for talking to me. And if you remember anything about Phillip, or anything you saw this morning, please let me know."

Tommy went outside for the tray and wished he had more to offer than empty platitudes. Men like George seemed to have been forgotten by the country since they returned. They had been asked to do a job under impossible circumstances, and then left to their own misery when their work was done.

A feeling of almost overwhelming powerlessness threatened to wash over Tommy.

Fortunately he was saved from his helplessness as a crash sounded downstairs and furious shouting had him running down the stairs to see what had happened.

***

"What on earth—" Tommy's words were cut off as he saw Mrs Warren, Elsie's mother, standing in the middle of the pub shrieking unintelligibly while shaking Evelyn roughly by the shoulders.

Partridge was doing his best to extricate Evelyn from the larger woman's hands whilst Evelyn spoke in a calming voice. The din Mrs Warren was making made it impossible for Tommy to hear what she was saying.

Tommy grasped Mrs Warren's hands and removed them from Evelyn and propelled the woman away from his wife. "Mrs Warren, what is the meaning of this?"

"Elsie!" the woman sobbed. "That man is trying to kill my Elsie."

Now was not the time to explain to Mrs Warren that grabbing hold of Evelyn and screaming incoherently was not helping her daughter.

"Are they at your house?"

Mrs Warren nodded. "Please help her!"

Partridge followed Tommy to the door and both men pulled on their boots and coats as they hurried out of the pub. As they reached the garden gate to Elsie's home, Tommy slipped on the icy path. He grabbed the gate post to keep himself upright.

A moment later, he rushed through the front door of the house he had visited earlier with Evelyn. In the kitchen they found Elsie laying on the floor with Len standing over her.

"What have you done, man?" Tommy barked at him.

Leonard Williams stared at his hands. "She had to be silenced."

Tommy knelt next to Elsie and put his fingers against her neck. The imprints of Len's fingers were easily discernible against the white column of her throat. "There's a pulse!"

"I'll go for Dr Mainwaring." Partridge stared at the still form of Elsie.

"Better to try Dr Wilder first," Tommy instructed. He turned to Len. "Why? Why did you think this was necessary."

"She had been nattering to you. It was only a matter of time before my Dorothy got wind of the filth she was saying."

Tommy sighed. "She admitted only to a kiss in an alcove near the entrance to the church. That is obviously not acceptable for a married man, who is also a churchwarden, but I don't think it classifies as filth."

"I am unclean. I am dirty." Len paced the length of the small kitchen, looked at Tommy, and then began his agitated steps. "I have had immoral and impure thoughts and deeds. I will go to Hell."

Tommy thought it was more probable that Len would go to Hell, if such a thing existed, because he had half killed Elsie and not because of his adulterous behaviour. "Calm down, Len. I'm sure the vicar will listen to you, should you wish to unburden yourself to him. As I'm sure you know, he's an extremely understanding and wise man."

"How will that help Dorothy?" Len sneered. "She will make my life a living hell."

Tommy chose not to voice his opinion that would take a complete role reversal as far as he could tell. From what he had witnessed earlier that day, it seemed that it was poor Dorothy Williams who led a far from ideal life with Len choosing to do what he wanted, when he wanted.

Len's words were all about himself—he had showed no concern for Elsie, or for his wife beyond how it would impact him. Tommy had barely paid him a moment's attention all the times he had attended church. Len Williams had seemed a meek, quiet, and insignificant man. He was now showing himself to have hidden and alarming depths.

He had to consider the possibility that Phillip had come across Len and Elsie in the church that morning. Perhaps Len had lured Phillip outside with the promise of money if he kept quiet about what he had seen. That didn't explain how Len was able to cut Phillip's throat unless he had carried a knife to church with him.

No, the conclusion they had drawn earlier that the murder was a premeditated act made the most sense.

Now, of course, there was the issue of what he would do with Len once Elsie had been taken care of. Under ordinary circumstances the police would attend and take Len away to be questioned—most likely for attempted murder. These were extraordinary conditions and Tommy would have to think of something equally as rare to ensure law and order was maintained.

Reg hurried in then and began to examine Elsie.

Tommy pulled Partridge to one side while keeping an eye on Len. "I know this might be a lot to ask, but I have a job for you."

"Of course, My Lord," Partridge answered. "I will do whatever you need me to."

"You may change your mind when you find out what it is." Tommy's mouth quirked up in a half smile.

Partridge shrugged. "I doubt it."

"We will have to lock up Len," Tommy whispered.

"Lock up?" Partridge echoed. "Is there a dungeon under the manor house I don't know about?"

"That would be the easy answer. Unfortunately, there is nothing like that at Hessleham Hall, or anywhere else in the village, to my knowledge."

"Then how shall we do it?"

"The rooms at the pub lock. I will ask Mr and Mrs Hughes if we are able to use one of their rooms to contain Len until the police get here."

"And my role in this would be?" Partridge raised an eyebrow.

Tommy smiled apologetically. "Jailer."

" I can do that," the estate manager answered immediately.

"Check up on him, take him food, that type of thing. Are you certain that is acceptable?"

"My Lord," Partridge answered. "You gave me a second chance when many employers would've shown me the door. That faith is something I can never repay in any other way than my deeds."

Tommy clapped Partridge on the back. "I appreciate your willingness in these desperate times."

Reg looked up at Tommy then. "We need to get this woman into a bed. Hopefully once she is in a warm, comfortable environment she will make a full recovery. There isn't anything I can do to speed that outcome along, unfortunately."

"Right," Partridge said as he approached Len. "You are coming with me!"

Len looked at the much bigger man and, to Tommy's surprise, nodded meekly. "I deserve punishment."

"Can I trust you to walk alongside me?" Partridge asked. "I should warn you that if you try to run, I will chase you, and I will catch you. Then I am likely to lock you in a coal cellar with no food and water, and not in a nice warm comfortable room in the Dog and Duck!"

Len picked up a coat and red scarf from the back of a kitchen chair but kept his eyes on the floor. "I'll go willingly."

"We will take Elsie to the pub and set up a bed for her in the pub," Tommy said. "Her mother can care for her there."

Reg found a blanket in the parlour and they wrapped Elsie as best they could before Tommy picked her up and they began the walk back to the pub.

Chapter Nine

"Oh, my poor baby," Mrs Warren whimpered as Tommy carried Elsie through the door. She caught sight of Len and dashed over to him. "What have you done to my child? My poor innocent child."

"Innocent," Len hissed. "Not nearly as innocent as you think!"

Mrs Warren gasped. "What do you mean?" She turned her gaze onto Tommy. "What does he mean?"

"I really don't know, Mrs Warren," Tommy soothed. "I think he has gone quite mad."

Partridge quickly ushered Len to the door marked 'private' before he could say anything more.

"Is he the one?" Her eyes went wide. "Did he kill Mr Newley and then attack my Elsie?"

"It is too soon to know that for sure."

"Now then, Mrs Warren." Reg stepped forward. "Give Lord Northmoor some space. "I believe the best thing to do right now is to get Elsie comfortable on a makeshift bed down here so we can keep an eye on her. I am sure you will want to be calm and reassuring when she regains consciousness?"

"Of course, Doctor," Mrs Warren replied meekly.

"I will go speak to Mrs Hughes," Evelyn said. "Shall I make her aware you appear to be using her pub as a temporary jail, or will you be doing that?"

Tommy's lips twitched at her cheek. "I will go and speak to her when we have Elsie settled. I do hope she isn't too put out."

"Whyever would she be that?" Evelyn asked as she walked towards the door that led to the upstairs rooms. "We have commandeered her establishment as a central point for our investigation, brought in a man we have no authority to detain, and are now turning the lounge area of her pub into a makeshift hospital."

"When you put it like that, we are rather taking liberties, aren't we?"

"She is a reasonable woman." Evelyn thought it was time she stopped teasing her husband. "I am sure she will understand."

Evelyn explained the situation with regards to Elsie to Mrs Hughes and asked if she could spare clean linens to make up a temporary bed for the unconscious woman.

As the two women, their arms full of blankets, pillows, and sheets came out of the store cupboard they met Partridge coming out of one of the rooms. He locked the door and pocketed the key.

"What is going on?" Mrs Hughes demanded.

"Ah." Evelyn and Partridge shared a guilt laden glance. "I believe Lord Northmoor has something he would like to discuss with you."

"He does, does he?" Mrs Hughes added her burden to Evelyn's. "You had better help me get a mattress from one of the beds I have left and bring it downstairs where I believe it is required."

"Yes, Mrs Hughes." Partridge followed the woman along the corridor leaving Evelyn to take her armful of bedding downstairs.

As soon as Elsie was settled between crisp, clean white sheets, Tommy took Mrs Hughes through to the kitchen. Reg knelt next to his patient and went through a series of checks.

"Will she be alright?" Mrs Warren asked anxiously.

"I cannot see any reason why she shouldn't make a full recovery." Reg reassured her. "She is a very lucky woman to have not suffered more serious harm."

"Why would Leonard Williams do such a thing?" Mrs Warren's worried eyes found Evelyn's.

"I think that is a conversation for you to have with your daughter when she is recovered," Evelyn said. "Now perhaps everyone would like something to eat?"

"I'm famished," Partridge admitted.

"I shall go home for dinner," Reg said. "I will come back in two to three hours. However, if Miss Warren's condition changes, please come and fetch me."

Mrs Warren said she was not up to eating but may take a bowl of soup later when Elsie was well enough to join her in a meal.

Evelyn waited outside the kitchen door until Mrs Hughes came out.

"Oh!" she said, startled. "Lady Northmoor, you didn't have to wait until we had finished speaking. You surely know everything your husband had to tell me."

"I didn't wish to interrupt." Evelyn grinned at the other woman. "I wasn't sure if you were telling Tommy he's horribly presumptuous taking over your pub like this."

"Completely the opposite." Mrs Hughes patted Evelyn's hand. "I have told your husband that the village is very lucky that a man such as him is willing to investigate this matter. If the old earl were still alive, he would be back at the manor with not a thought or worry as to the fate of the villagers."

"It is very kind of you to be so understanding,"

"Not at all, Lady Northmoor." Mrs Hughes walked past Evelyn towards the door to the upstairs. "By the way, please pass on my regards to your cook. Her soup was quite excellent and has perked George up no end."

Evelyn went through to the kitchen. "I fear we may need another hamper full of food just for Partridge."

"Come here," Tommy said softly.

She moved into his arms and rested her head on his chest. "I am sorry for being so irritable earlier."

"This last five months has been rather tricky for both us to navigate." He kissed the top of her head. "The expectations for us have changed dramatically. It is only to be expected that we should experience some teething troubles."

"You are always so reasonable!" she exclaimed.

"Would you rather I wasn't?" Tommy moved back a step and looked at Evelyn. "Should I scold you and tell you that sometimes your words wound me?"

Evelyn raised up on her tiptoes and pressed her lips to his. "Yes, you should. We should always be honest with each other. Especially about the difficult things. If we don't have that in our marriage, then I fear for the future."

"Fear no more, Mrs Christie," Tommy said, waltzing Evelyn around the kitchen. "Our marriage is safe with me."

Evelyn knew she was lucky every single day that she spent with Tommy. Even though he often infuriated her, there was no better man she could have chosen to spend the rest of her life with.

Tommy was well aware that by referring to her as 'Mrs Christie' would remind her of an easier time in their life—when they were simply a young married couple and not two people attempting to adjust to being Lord and Lady Northmoor. She found the stifling responsibilities and expectations so much harder to bear than he did.

"Let us put together a cold supper." Evelyn pulled the hamper towards her. "Like we used to back in the cottage."

"Only instead of it being just us two, we will share our meal time with our estate manager, an unconscious woman and her mother, with a prisoner upstairs with the landlord and landlady of the pub."

"It is rather queer how things have turned out in our lives, isn't it?"

"I would prefer it if people didn't keep dropping dead around us," Tommy agreed. "But let us forget about this ghastly murder for now. We will have a good night's sleep and then see if we can start piecing things together in the morning."

***

The following morning, Tommy slipped down to the kitchen and brought a tea tray up to their room.

"We can't lay in bed all day." Evelyn accepted a cup of tea. "We're not at home now. Everyone will think we are being exceedingly lazy."

"I don't care," Tommy responded, slipping back under the covers. "We know we are working up here where we cannot be overheard. That is good enough for me."

"Alright, let's get to work." Evelyn put her saucer on the bedside table and wrapped her hands around her cup. "We should start with what we know to be true."

101

"We know Phillip was killed between roughly eight and ten twenty yesterday morning because of the footprints and the fact the snow stopped falling around eight."

"There are a number of people with a motive to kill Phillip for differing reasons. We think it unlikely that someone killed him before church because even though the weather was inclement, the path to the church would have been busy with villagers clearing the snow from outside their houses and making their way to service. Someone either going behind the church or appearing from that direction would have looked exceedingly suspicious."

"Indeed," Evelyn agreed. "Especially after Phillip's body was found. So, although this isn't something we know for a fact, we are deducing that Phillip was killed in that narrow window of time when everyone was preoccupied with Alfred."

"Lots of people left the church at that time and had the means and opportunity," Tommy added. "Let's list them."

"Teddy has the best motive, but we cannot be sure he was where he said he was at the time of the murder. Ellen went off to the shop to fetch smelling salts."

"Do we think she is a viable suspect?" Tommy raised his eyebrows, scepticism clear in his eyes.

"Don't be such a chauvinist, Tommy Christie!" Evelyn admonished. "Women are more than capable of committing murder."

"By poisoning, or some other *gentle* method," Tommy argued. "Not by getting behind someone and cold bloodedly slitting their throat."

Evelyn shuddered. "It is particularly ghastly. And, you're right, it's more likely to be a man but I don't think we should rule Ellen out simply because she is a woman."

"What motive would she have?"

"I see you are determined to clear Miss Armstrong." Evelyn smiled indulgently. "Is that because she makes better jam even than Cook and you don't want her to be guilty because your breakfast isn't complete without a slathering of strawberry jam on toast?"

"It's jolly delicious." Tommy sipped his tea. "But there is a distinct lack of motive."

Evelyn looked at him pensively. "Percy suggested she was in love with Teddy."

"Well that sorts that out then,"

"Does it?"

"Of course." Tommy nodded. "If she's in love with Teddy, she wouldn't bump off Phillip because that now leaves Isolde free to pursue a relationship with Teddy. Ellen would have wanted Phillip to stay in the picture and hoped Teddy got bored of waiting for Isolde to be free."

"You're forgetting the unknown," Evelyn reminded him. "She should remain on the list of suspects because we don't yet have all the information we need to solve this."

"Alright, you win." Tommy grinned. "Who is next?"

"Annie came back to the pub to pull a pint of beer. That always struck me as a very odd thing to do."

"But she then explained to us that she used that as an excuse, she was really looking for George. Who, of course, must stay on the list even though it pains me to say so."

Evelyn finished her tea and rested the cup in the saucer. "Annie told us that Phillip was blackmailing her to let him stay here free. The insinuation was that George did not know this. But what if he did?"

"Again that is missing information. I wouldn't want to ask him that question outright, unless really necessary. If he didn't know, finding out might tip him back over the edge."

"Is there more tea in that pot?" she enquired.

"As you have not left bed to check, does that mean you wish me to pour you another cup?"

"If you wouldn't mind."

"Lady Northmoor, I do believe you are getting rather too accustomed to being waited upon." Tommy teased.

"Lord Northmoor, I believe you know from John's sermons that God looks favourably on those who help others."

Tommy chuckled. "I am not at all sure the almighty, or John, had in mind a husband fetching tea for his wife."

Evelyn held out her cup. "Do hurry, darling, I'm struggling to finish off our discussion because my throat is so dry."

"We should keep Len on the list." Tommy moved over to the tray he had set on the dressing table and poured them both another cup of tea. "Although Elsie didn't think he had time to slip outside and kill Phillip, you didn't see him come back in, did you?"

Evelyn shook her head. "I didn't. Aunt Em only mentioned seeing Elsie because she noticed she had her hat on. Now we know Elsie was with Len, we should ask her about Len directly."

He passed the fresh cup of tea over to her. "Is that everyone?"

"No, not long before George came in, Percy went to the vicarage to get Violet Rogers a cup of tea because she was practically hysterical."

"We must speak to Violet and Alfred this morning. Then Percy and Ellen. Hopefully we will find out some of the information that seems to be missing."

"The discussions we have had this morning seem to suggest this is a crime of opportunity." Evelyn frowned, frustrated at the contradictions in the case.

"Which makes a nonsense of our previous belief that this crime was premeditated. It can't be both." Tommy shook his head in consternation. "But as no one could predict Alfred having his fainting fit, they wouldn't have been able to plan a murder."

"And we think it was premeditated because the murderer must have arranged to meet Phillip and they brought a weapon to that meeting?" Evelyn clarified.

"Hurry with that tea, Evelyn," Tommy coaxed. "I'm jolly keen to find out more so this investigation makes sense."

Chapter Ten

Tommy and Evelyn left the pub a short while later. Breakfast had been a rather unsubstantial meal of bread and butter. Mrs Warren had informed them that Elsie had regained consciousness in the night. Reg had visited that morning and repeated his belief that she would make a full recovery.

Hopefully Elsie would be awake when they had finished the visits that had planned for that morning. Evelyn strongly believed the illicit relationship Len was having with Elsie was not the only reason he had become so aggressive the previous evening. After she had been scared so terribly, and with Len now locked away, perhaps Elsie would feel she was able to tell them the full story.

Partridge had informed them it had been a quiet night with their prisoner. He had eaten a little food that morning and mostly seemed very subdued, though had not demanded to leave the room as they had feared he may.

They arrived at Alfred's cottage, with neither Evelyn nor Tommy knowing much about the brother and sister. Their only plan was to speak to

Alfred and Violet separately and to ask general questions.

The door was answered soon after Tommy's knock, as though Alfred had been standing on the other side waiting.

"Goodness…My…Lord Northmoor," he stammered.

"Good morning, Mr Cross," Tommy said pleasantly. "We thought we would pop by and see how you have been since the unfortunate incident yesterday morning."

"How very kind, I am quite recovered. Thank you for asking." Alfred stood back from the door. "Won't you please come in? Violet is in the kitchen with the children. Shall I ask her to put the kettle on?"

"Please don't trouble yourselves on our account," Tommy said. "Perhaps if I could just have a quick word with you in private, Lady Northmoor can keep Violet company in the kitchen?"

For one moment, Tommy thought the other man was going to refuse. However, he collected himself, drew back his shoulders and indicated a door to the right. "Should I see you through to the kitchen, Lady Northmoor?"

Tommy glanced around the neat entrance. A coat stand stood to the left of the front door holding a man and a woman's coat and a bright red scarf. Underneath stood a pair of boots and an umbrella in a bucket.

"Just at the end of this passage, is it, Mr Cross?" Evelyn clarified. "I'm sure I shall manage, thank you."

"This is rather unexpected, if you don't mind my saying."

"We're talking to everyone," Tommy said lightly.

"Officially?" Alfred peered closely at Tommy as though he would be able to see the answer to his question on Tommy's face. "Take a seat."

"Thank you. I'm not in the police force anymore." Tommy sat on the worn brown armchair Alfred had designated. "I am here only in a civic capacity."

Alfred visibly relaxed. "I assume you have something specific to ask as you said you wanted privacy?"

"It's about Phillip Newley," Tommy leaned forward as though about to share a secret. "The victim."

"Oh yes?" Alfred mirrored Tommy's position as though he was eager to help.

"I don't know if you are aware, but sadly money has been going missing recently from the collection plate." Tommy looked at the door as though the next part of his sentence was top secret and he was afraid someone would overhear. "I wondered if, perhaps, you thought it could have been Phillip Newley who was taking the money. He was rather roguish, you know. Only very recently out of prison."

"I was aware of the missing money." Alfred rubbed his chin, as though giving the matter his utmost consideration. "I think you are correct, and it could well have been Newley. It started going missing about the time he turned up now I come to think about it."

"Dreadful situation." Tommy shook his head sadly. "The vicar is most distressed about it. I understand Percy Armstrong has been putting pressure on him to get the matter resolved."

"Perhaps with Mr Newley's unfortunate demise, that will be an end to it." Alfred pulled out a handkerchief and patted his forehead.

Tommy looked at the coals in the fireplace. They were glowing red, but there were no flames to warm Alfred's face enough to make him sweat.

"I expect you're right." Tommy sat back in his chair and crossed his ankles. "Was your sister particularly upset about Mr Newley's death?"

Alfred's face reddened further. "What do you mean? Violet? Why would she be? Whatever do you mean?"

Tommy paused, leaving a long silence that he could see was making Alfred even more nervous. He could almost see the apprehension swirling in Alfred's mind as he questioned what, and how much, Tommy could possibly know.

"Oh, I am sorry." Tommy gave an awkward little shrug. "Maybe I have got it wrong. I had understood that your sister and Phillip were 'walking out'. Is that the correct term?"

"Gosh." Alfred's right knee started jigging up and down. "I shouldn't have thought so. She is a war widow, you know."

Tommy tilted his head sympathetically to one side. "She must be desperately sad without her husband. And those poor children without their father. Is it perhaps possible she was searching for love again?"

"Lord Northmoor, I don't know where you have heard this quite *scandalous* rumour, but I am certain it is incorrect." Alfred mopped his brow.

"I do apologise if I have caused offence."

"My sister is a good woman. It is true that she has struggled financially since she lost her husband but if she were ready for love again, it most certainly would not be with another woman's husband I assure you."

"Indeed." Tommy nodded in a way he hoped conveyed sympathy. "I can't think how I could have understood this situation wrongly. I say, doesn't your sister qualify for a pension?"

Alfred looked away, his Adam's apple bobbed in his throat, and his face changed from an angry mottled red to a hue as white as he had been the day before when he collapsed in the church.

"Are you quite well?" Tommy leaned over as though to pat Alfred's arm.

The other man recoiled from his touch and stared at Tommy with fire burning in his eyes. "You think you're so clever."

"I am very sorry if I've upset you, that was not my intention."

"Violet cannot get a widow's pension because, as I am sure you already know, her husband was shot for cowardice."

"I did not know that," Tommy whispered, feeling desperately sad. He had known the realities of war himself and didn't think anyone should have the power to judge another man's bravery unless they had themselves walked, or marched, or fought, a day in that man's shoes.

"Well, there you have it." Alfred spread his arms wide. "Our family skeleton is well and truly out of the closet."

"You have my word that I will not repeat what you have told me. I do not believe that it is pertinent to the investigation."

"Now, see here," Alfred said belligerently. "You said that you were here out of civic duty. Now you are calling what you are doing an investigation. I do not think your word can be trusted."

He'd rather walked into that one. Tommy couldn't see any way out of the hole he had dug. He had allowed his sentiment to get in the way of his interview with Alfred and made a hash of it.

Tommy hoped that Evelyn was having more luck than he'd had.

Evelyn knocked on the open door of the kitchen. "So sorry to barge in like this, Mrs Rogers."

"Lady Northmoor!" Violet's hands covered her mouth. "I wasn't expecting visitors. Please excuse the place. The children…"

"Mrs Rogers, I assure you, I haven't come to inspect your home. Your kitchen looks very warm and inviting. I'm sure that's why the children enjoy playing in here." Evelyn looked around the room. Violet had arranged some sheets over a couple of the kitchen chairs, and it appeared the children were sitting under the table in their 'tent'.

"It's not my home," Violet said, sinking down into one of the available chairs. "It's Alfred's. He is letting me, and kiddies stay here because…"

Evelyn sat in the chair at a right angle to Violet. "You don't have to tell me if you don't want to, but I am a very good listener."

"But you're…you wouldn't understand."

"You won't know until you try me."

Violet looked at the open kitchen door, as though Alfred would be cross if he heard her talking about her personal business. "I couldn't pay the rent on the house I shared with my late husband."

A deep blush flooded the woman's cheeks, and she turned her face away in shame.

"Mrs Rogers, you will not be the only woman in this country who has to live with relatives because times have become difficult for her. That is what family is for, is it not?"

Violet smiled tentatively. "That's what Alfred says."

"Well, there we are then. You have absolutely nothing to be embarrassed for."

"I feel quite dreadful," Violet confided. "Alfred has a second job. I know he has because he slips me extra money now and again on top of the housekeeping. He says it's so the kiddies don't go without."

"What does Alfred do for work?"

"He helps out at one of the local farms. It doesn't pay much. He was barely managing to feed himself and keep a roof over his own head before we moved in. That's why I know the dear man is working another job to keep us."

"No wonder you were so desperately upset yesterday when he took ill."

"Oh, My Lady!" Violet exclaimed. "I thought I was going to lose him. It's a dreadful thing to say while he was laying on the floor but all I could think was if he died it would mean the workhouse for me and the children. I just couldn't bear the thought."

"Surely things would not be as desperate as all that?" Evelyn's stomach rumbled. Whatever was cooking in the homely kitchen smelled wonderful, a timely reminder that bread and butter was not an adequate meal, regardless how many people managed to survive on less. "An attractive woman such as yourself must have young men queuing down the lane wanting to court you?"

"I couldn't entertain fellas." Violet shook her head decisively. "Not so soon after losing my Harold."

"You kissed that man in the park, Mam!" A gleeful voice floated out from under the table.

"Minnie Rogers, what a terrible thing to say about your own mother." Violet wouldn't meet Evelyn's gaze and she got the impression the other woman now wished she had sent her children upstairs to play while they chatted.

"You did though, Mam." A boy spoke this time. "And said you would buy us sweets at Mr Armstrong's shop if we didn't tell."

"I…" Violet's bottom lip wobbled.

"Mrs Rogers," Evelyn said calmly. "I already know all about Mr Newley and yourself, so you do not need to trouble yourself about your children's indiscreet chatter on my account."

"You know?" Violet pulled a hankie out of the sleeve of her plain wool dress and blew her nose noisily. "No one knows."

"You live in Hessleham," Evelyn said, as though that should explain everything. "There isn't much that goes on in this village that isn't chatted about in the shops, then repeated and expanded upon the next day. You must know that."

"Phillip said we must keep it a secret. He didn't want that wife of his claiming money from him after the divorce. Especially when she would get nicely set up with that doctor once she was free."

"I didn't know Phillip was going to divorce Isolde," Evelyn kept her voice low and understanding, hoping Violet would fill in the gaps in her knowledge.

"Wouldn't you divorce her if you were him?" Violet spat. "The lies that woman told about him, then she wouldn't even give him somewhere to stay when he came to give her his forgiveness. I am quite horrified that a woman such as that teaches my children."

"That sounds positively dreadful."

"Imagine how devastated Phillip was when he arrived to find she had besmirched his name with outright fabrications. He was just mortified to hear that people believed he had been in prison." Violet lowered her eyes to the table. "I happened to meet him one day near the pond and he told me how lovely it was to have someone to talk to who really

113

understands him. We didn't mean for anything to develop between us, but he was so relieved to have someone who believed in him. And I allowed myself to be flattered. He was a very attractive man."

Personally, Evelyn had found him oily and supercilious as well as having an overinflated opinion of himself. She forced a conciliatory smile onto her face. "I can see how that would happen, definitely."

What she meant was she could see how Phillip had created a situation where Violet had fallen for his dubious charms and web of lies.

Violet sobbed into her handkerchief. "We were going to be married, you know."

"Oh, I am so sorry, you poor thing." Evelyn shuffled her chair nearer and patted Violet's shoulder. "How very shattering for you to lose your fiancé in such an horrific way."

"You do understand. I really didn't think you would." Violet shook her head in wonder. "You see why no one must know we were engaged, don't you?"

"It is no one else's business," Evelyn said firmly.

"Not even Alfred knows." Violet wiped tears from her cheeks. "I feel terrible keeping it a secret from him after all he has done for me, but Phillip insisted that until he had things sorted out with *that woman* we had to meet in secret."

Sympathy for Isolde flooded through Evelyn. Her snake of a husband was begging for her forgiveness and all the while, he was cosying up to the gullible and impressionable Violet.

"You have my very deepest sympathies, my dear."

"I should imagine when the police get here, they will be taking that doctor away and he'll be swinging from the end of a rope by Easter." Violet seemed to remember that her children were in the room and she slapped a hand over her mouth.

"You think Dr Mainwaring killed Mr Newley?"

"*Everyone* thinks so. He's desperately in love with her, but that one loves no one but herself. Mark my words, she will come unstuck when the school board hears about her behaviour."

"Behaviour?" Evelyn enquired as innocently as she could. Just because Nora had not heard any gossip in relation to Isolde and Teddy did not mean there was none.

"Like I said, the lies about Phillip. And refusing to give shelter to her own husband. Shameful."

"Indeed." Evelyn got to her feet. Whether Tommy was finished or not, she needed to go before she spoke some of the home truths that were on the very tip of her tongue. "Thank you so much for our little chat. I do hope you will soon recover from this terrible ordeal."

Chapter Eleven

"I have never heard anything quite so ridiculous in all my days." Evelyn closed the garden gate behind her gently, even though she wanted to slam it she was so frustrated. "Phillip had Violet convinced he was the injured party."

"She believed him?"

"Every word. He even convinced her he had never been to prison."

"Clever fellow."

"He was despicable," Evelyn retorted. "No wonder Isolde needed the comfort of a lovely upstanding and honest man such as Teddy."

"Now, Evelyn, we do not know that she has spent time receiving comfort from Teddy."

"I do wish Teddy had an alibi that we could be certain of."

"It would make this investigation easier. It's not at all pleasant suspecting one's friends of a heinous crime."

Evelyn sighed. "I suppose we had better visit the Armstrong siblings and see if they have anything to add."

"Percy is a most disagreeable fellow."

"Is he?" Evelyn enquired. "I've always found him very eager to please."

"Too eager. He makes me feel quite uncomfortable."

"Let's put him towards the top of our list."

Tommy put his arm around Evelyn and pulled her closer. "Sarcasm does not suit you, darling."

"Really?" Evelyn giggled. "I think I'm rather good at it."

"It would be handy if the culprit were Percy or Alfred. Or anyone else, really, who is not Teddy."

"Percy has no motive that I can discern."

"Alfred mentioned Violet's husband was shot as a coward so that explains why she does not receive a widow's pension. However, you've said she was set to marry Phillip which would mean Alfred would be able to give up his second job and not have to support Violet and her children which gives him no motive."

"Unless he saw through Phillip and killed him to save Violet's honour or something equally noble."

Tommy squeezed Evelyn's shoulder. "That doesn't work because we are forgetting that Alfred was on the floor of the church at the time we believe the murder occurred. That rather rules him out."

"Let us stop tying ourselves in knots trying to work this thing out." Evelyn approached the Armstrongs' shop. "Now, do you think we should knock at the shop door or will there be another entrance to their private quarters at the rear?"

"I can't imagine that Percy won't be in the shop even though it doesn't seem to be open. Just in case someone wants something, he will want to be available."

"Do you think people will be so foolhardy as to visit the village shop when there is a murderer on the loose?"

"If they need some tobacco for their pipe, or the morning paper, or just want to see who has heard what, I'm certain they will."

Tommy peered through the window and then turned back round to Evelyn. "I was right, he's doing something with a clipboard."

"Hurry up and knock, then, it must be warmer in there than it is out here."

"Don't need to." Tommy grinned. "He has seen me and is hurrying over to unlock the door."

Evelyn squeezed his hand. "Be nice."

The door opened and Percy invited them inside in his usual over solicitous way. "Do come inside. Should we go upstairs to the parlour to talk. It would be so much more cosy than down here. Do excuse me, I am taking the opportunity of an unexpected day off to do a stock take."

"We don't need to go upstairs, Percy, we're happy to talk down here. However, we would like to speak to your sister too."

"Ellen?" Percy's face took on the same unpleasant look Evelyn had noticed in the church when he had commented on Ellen's feelings for Teddy. "Why would you need to speak to her?"

"We're speaking to everyone."

"I can tell you where she was without you needing to bother her, Lord Northmoor."

Evelyn cringed as the man practically bowed at Tommy's feet. She could see clearly what her husband meant about the man. It interested her more, however, that he seemed to be reluctant to let them speak to Ellen.

"I appreciate that." Tommy stepped nearer to Percy. The much shorter shopkeeper visibly cowered away from him. "I have a job to do until the police get here, and to do it properly I must speak to everyone individually. Unless, of course, you think your sister has something to hide and that's the reason for your reluctance?"

"Goodness gracious me!" Percy squeaked. "Of course not. I simply thought Ellen would probably be knitting or something and not want to be interrupted in case she loses her place. You know how women are."

"We will wait here while you fetch her."

As soon as Evelyn heard Percy's soft tread on the stairs, she turned to Tommy. "Do you think he doesn't want us to speak to Ellen for a particular reason or do you think he just thinks she's unimportant because she's a woman?"

"I really don't know," Tommy answered.

"There's something about him I do not like."

"Ssh," Tommy admonished. "He will hear you."

"He seems terrified of you."

Tommy shrugged. "In awe, I think. It's very tiresome. I am the same man as I was before I became Lord Northmoor. I detest how people treat me differently."

Footsteps sounded again on the stairs behind the shop counter and Percy reappeared with his sister. "I was right. She was knitting."

Ellen looked flustered. "Percy says you need to speak to us, but I really don't know why. I didn't see a thing. I can't think…"

"You're babbling again," Percy said sternly.

"Anything you may have seen while you were getting the smelling salts would be very useful." Tommy smiled at the nervous woman. "If you saw anyone while you were walking here or heard anyone running away. Anything at all may be useful, even if you think it has no relevance."

"Nothing at all," Ellen replied quickly.

"Please take your time to think carefully. Maybe there were footprints in the snow somewhere you wouldn't expect?"

Ellen shook her head. "I'm sorry, My Lord, I would like to help you but I came into the shop and got the smelling salts and went straight back to the church. I didn't see anyone."

"As I told you." Percy's smile was smug. "I couldn't even get the infernal woman at the vicarage to answer the door. But, of course, that is not unusual."

"You didn't see the vicar? He had gone out to bring blankets for Alfred. Surely your paths must have crossed?" Evelyn asked.

"I didn't see him." Percy shook his head decisively. "Definitely not. Of course, he detested Phillip Newley because he's fond of Isolde Newley. Had to ask her to leave the shop once because Newley was going on at her. Not good for business, you understand."

"Are you suggesting the vicar may have killed Mr Newley?"

Percy lifted a shoulder. "I didn't say that. But village gossip is that he would do anything for her."

"I…I don't know if this is relevant," Ellen stammered over her words and looked doubtfully at her brother.

"Oh, Ellen, really. Are you going to repeat something you heard over the shop counter?"

"You just did," Ellen said, in a rare show of bravado. She quickly turned to face Tommy. "There's also talk that there was an enormous row between the doctor and Mr Newley outside the pub on the Friday night before the murder. Apparently, Dr Mainwaring was overheard offering Mr Newley money to leave the village."

"Goodness, Ellen, you will get the doctor into trouble saying things like that." Percy looked at his sister aghast. "I thought you were fond of him?"

Ellen looked stricken. She stared at Percy, then back at Evelyn and Tommy. Finally, the realisation of what she had said seemed too much for her and she fled past the counter with a sob.

"What did you make of that?"

"I'm glad he's not my brother." Tommy pulled a face. "What a perfectly horrid man. That poor girl living there."

"She's hardly a girl, Tommy! I've often wondered why she never married. I think I now have my answer."

"Back to the pub we go. Let's hope Elsie is awake now."

"What should we do after that?"

"I have a little idea," Tommy said.

Evelyn bumped him with her hip. "I am the one who generally has little ideas."

"You haven't had one for a while, so I thought I should."

"What is your idea? Will I like it?"

"It involves us getting fed properly." Tommy waggled his eyebrows at her. "I am so hungry I can barely think straight."

"That's because you usually devour at least four sausages every morning on top of heaps of scrambled eggs and bacon. Finished off with toast and Miss Armstrong's strawberry jam."

Tommy patted his stomach. "Two slices of slightly stale bread and butter were a very poor substitute."

"How do you intend to organise a meal?"

"Reg wants to keep an eye on Elsie. Milly needs bed rest and help with the children. I thought you could accompany them back to the house. Whilst you are there, I am certain Mrs O'Connell will have a great deal of sympathy for a starving earl and refill that hamper."

Evelyn thought through Tommy's suggestion. It made a lot of sense. "Are you thinking Milly may employ Elsie as a nursemaid?"

Tommy held out his hands. "If that was to happen, it would be a very good arrangement all round wouldn't it? Elsie worked well at the vicarage but needs guidance, and who better than Milly to provide that?"

"That is inspired, Tommy, what a wonderful suggestion."

"So if they all go to the manor together, Mrs O'Connell can feed Milly, Elsie can help with the children, and they can test the arrangement."

"Have you mentioned this to Reg?"

Tommy nodded. "This morning, while I was making the tea tray. He thinks it's a wonderful idea. He will come back with you and I thought perhaps you might want to bring your little friend with you?"

"Davey?"

"Of course, who else?" he smiled at her. "He was rather useful last year when he found that bloody handkerchief outside the pub."

"You think he can find the knife?"

He shrugged. "It won't hurt to try. Especially if we don't have any more snow. If the murderer has thrown it somewhere, it should be easier to find."

"We haven't explored the possibility that the murderer kept the knife with them, cleaned it and put it back where it belongs."

"That would be dangerous, it would be full of blood that would then get on their clothes."

"Not if they cleaned it in the snow first."

"Good point." Tommy considered her suggestion. "They could have thrown it over the hedge into the field beyond the churchyard. The police will have a lot of places to search when they arrive."

They arrived back at the pub. Evelyn was pleased to see Elsie sitting up in her makeshift bed. The colour was back in her face, though her neck was marred with ugly purple bruises.

"Miss Warren," Tommy said. "How pleased I am to see how well you look."

"Thank you, Lord Northmoor." Elsie's voice was hoarse and scratchy. "I expect you will want to ask me more questions."

"We were rather concerned that Len seemed to think that you needed shutting up. That does make us believe that there is something you may not have dared tell us. We're hoping you feel brave enough to share that information with us, especially now that you know Len is locked up." Evelyn hoped the young woman would feel reassured by her calm tone.

"He can't get out, can he?" she asked fearfully.

"You're quite safe here," Tommy reassured her. "However, we do have a proposal for you."

"What might that be?" Elsie looked unsure.

"My sister needs rest," Evelyn explained. "You may be aware that she is having a baby and already has three very energetic children. We are hoping that you would accompany them to the manor this afternoon and help care for the children. It gets both you and Milly out of the village until we can resolve the murder."

"I do like children." Elsie smiled. "I do believe I would feel safer at the house. Thank you for suggesting it, you're very kind."

"It was Tommy's idea actually." Evelyn was only too happy to give her husband the credit deserved for his plan.

"Oh goodness, what about Mother?"

"She shall go with you, if you would both like," Tommy said. "She will want to be sure that you are recovering properly."

"Lord Northmoor, I couldn't possibly do that. I could not impose."

"We insist," Evelyn said. "You are helping us, don't forget."

"It will be like having grandchildren again." Mrs Warren's eyes filled with tears.

Evelyn didn't want to ask the question as she could already see the heartache on the woman's face.

"My sister had children, but she moved to Hull when she married," Elsie explained. "She and her children were among the unfortunates who died in 1915 when an airship dropped its bombs."

Now was not an appropriate time to say that any attention Mrs Warren gave the children would be more than their actual grandmother, Evelyn's mother, had given the children in their lifetime.

"Wonderful!" Tommy clapped his hands together. "Mrs Warren, I would be pleased to accompany you to your house so you can pack some things for yourself and your daughter."

"Goodness, yes, and maybe a few little things for the children, too. How very exciting. I've never been to the manor." Mrs Warren chattered as she put on her coat and hat. "Of course, I've been to the fete that you have in the garden but that's not the same thing at all."

"I shall make sure that Mrs Chapman, she is our housekeeper, gives you a tour of the entire house. She is very proud of it."

"Lord Northmoor," Mrs Warren breathed. "I will be the envy of the whole village."

As soon as they left, Partridge excused himself to the kitchen and Evelyn moved to sit next to Elsie's bed. "Do you feel able to tell me what you were too afraid to say yesterday?"

"Len destroyed all the loyalty I had for him when he attacked me last night." Elsie trembled. "I was quite sure he was going to kill me. If Mother hadn't come into the kitchen when she did, I'm certain I would be dead."

"Did his attack stop when your mother came in?"

"I'm not sure. I remember hearing Mother's voice and that must have been when I passed out."

"What was Len so keen to stop you telling us?" Evelyn asked gently.

"He had an arrangement with Alfred Cross." Elsie's brow puckered. "I've been trying to think what it might be, but I cannot come up with anything. Len covered for Alfred and in return, Alfred made sure we were not gone too long. I think they had some sort of signal for each other, but I don't know what it was."

"Might Alfred have gone out earlier in the service?"

"I really don't know, I'm afraid," Elsie replied. "I sit at the back, but I always face front so as not to look suspicious. Len taps me on the back, and I go into our little place and he then follows."

"It would be possible for Alfred to have slipped out without your knowledge, then?"

"Oh, absolutely." Elsie nodded. "He could easily have done that."

"Thank you for telling me."

"Have I helped?" she asked eagerly.

"I wish I could say yes." Evelyn grimaced. "Unfortunately, I am more confused than ever."

Chapter Twelve

Evelyn travelled to the manor with Milly and her children. Reg would follow with Mrs Warren and Elsie. The journey was enjoyable with the children excited to be in what they saw as an old fashioned mode of transport.

It was strange for Evelyn to think that her niece and nephews would grow up in such a different world to the one she herself had enjoyed as a child. Motor cars were more convenient and becoming ever more common.

James' exuberance was curtailed only by Evelyn keeping a tight hold of the back of his trousers. Otherwise she was certain he would plummet into a ditch, he was leaning so far out of the carriage. Elsie would have her work cut out taking care of her nephew in the enormous manor house.

"I wonder how quickly Mrs Chapman can pack away everything that is breakable." Milly gave a wry grin.

"Oh, I should think she will put it all into the billiard room and lock the door," Evelyn said airily.

"How easily you said that."

"How do you mean?"

"Six months ago you would have been terrified at the idea of a broken glass or a chipped piece of china. Now you seem quite blasé about it."

Evelyn bit her lip. "Do you think that is a bad thing?"

"Not at all." Milly reached forward and patted Evelyn's hand. "I think it means you have finally found your place in life."

"I never thought I would find it at Hessleham Hall," Evelyn admitted. "Now it is hard to imagine living anywhere else."

The previous August Tommy had inherited both the manor house and his title, when his uncle and then his cousin had been murdered. Prior to that, Evelyn's visits to the grand house had been fraught with nerves and homesickness for their little cottage in the village.

"I like you a lot more than the previous Lady Northmoor." Milly grinned wickedly.

"Lillian seems so long ago. Although she actually only held that title for a short period of time, she had played at being 'lady of the manor' for years."

"And not very well," Milly commented with her usual frankness. "She was a quite dreadful person."

"I thought we might have heard from her. Perhaps a postcard from New York bragging about her wonderful new life."

"I think the film making tends to happen in Hollywood these days." Milly turned to smile at James who was excitedly pointing out a mountain hare, which was barely discernible in the snow. "I see it, dear, but you will not be able to catch it however hard you try. Please try to sit still, Aunt Evelyn's arms must be getting extremely tired keeping you from toppling out of the carriage."

"Are you very ill?"

"I'm more tired than usual this time," Milly admitted. "Of course, there is a reason for that."

Evelyn looked at James and nodded. "Yes, I understand that."

Milly followed her sister's gaze. "He is certainly a lot of work. Though he isn't the reason for my excessive tiredness."

"May I know the reason?"

"Of course," Milly took hold of Evelyn's hand. "It isn't a secret. I simply wasn't sure how much to share with you. Now you have asked the question, I shall tell you. Dr Mainwaring is fairly certain the reason I am as big as a barn and am experiencing so much fatigue is because I am having two babies."

"Goodness." Evelyn gulped. "Twins. No wonder you agreed to Elsie Warren helping and you staying at the manor for a little while. I didn't expect you to."

"Reg ordered me to agree." Milly admitted.

Ordinarily, Milly's mild mannered husband acquiesced to whatever his wife wanted. On the few occasions he felt the need to put his foot down, Milly knew he was serious and it was pointless arguing with him.

"I understood Dr Mainwaring called to see you because you didn't feel the baby move?"

"Not much room in there." Milly pulled a face. "They are making up for it today, though, elbows and knees everywhere."

Evelyn nodded, but was lost for words. She didn't know what to say because it wasn't something she had experienced herself. Milly had also tried to keep her from feeling just as she felt now by not sharing the news that there were two babies.

Swallowing back her own misery, she resolved to share in her sister's joy and make a better effort to be less self centred. "You could have told me, Milly, I am thrilled for you and Reg."

"I didn't want to upset you," Milly said. "You haven't seemed quite yourself lately. The last thing I would want is to cause you any further distress."

"You're my sister." Evelyn squeezed her sister's hand. "After the absolute horrors of our childhood, we are bonded even closer than other sisters."

Milly shrugged. "Mother did her best. It just wasn't her way to be demonstrative towards us. Plenty of children experience far worse childhoods than ours. We were fed and warm, that is something to be grateful for."

"She never did that herself, though, she always gave the chore of caring for us to someone else."

"Evelyn," her sister said sternly. "It was still done. I find it tiresome to look back on things I cannot change. What you must do is look forward and forge your own path with your children when they come. As they surely will."

"What if that never happens for me?" Evelyn hated the note of self pity that crept into her voice.

"Then you shall do what other smart, resourceful women do." Milly looked towards the manor house as it came into view. "Goodness only knows you have the means to do it."

"You're saying I should occupy myself with other things, do good for other people."

"Yes, now do pull yourself together, Evelyn. You have advantages that others can only dream of."

Malton opened the door as Partridge pulled the carriage as near to the steps leading up the house as he could. He peered enquiringly at the estate manager, then looked back at the carriage.

He moved forward and opened the door. Evelyn gripped her nephew more firmly to stop him falling onto Malton. "My Lady?"

"Malton, good morning." She passed James down to the butler.

"James, help your Aunt Evelyn down, please." Milly called to her son.

The five year old gallantly held out his hand to Evelyn, seven year old Leah came next, followed by two year old Samuel. As soon as his siblings, aunt, and mother were standing on the steps of the house, James took off running across the lawn.

"Malton!" Aunt Em's voice sounded from the drawing room. "Who does that child running across our lawn belong to?"

"Oh dear." Milly put a hand over her mouth to stifle a giggle. "Will he be in terrible trouble?"

"Of course not." Evelyn linked her arm through Milly's. "He is doing what little boys do. I am so glad you're here with me."

"Are you not going straight back to the village?"

"I am, but as soon as we have unmasked the villain, I shall be home, I am very much looking forward to spending time with you all."

Evelyn walked to the drawing room. She left Milly in the door and crossed the patterned rug to where Aunt Em sat in her favourite chair. Leaning forward, she kissed the older woman's cheek.

"You are still alive then, I was beginning to wonder?"

"Were you concerned I wasn't? You expected me to stay overnight in the village, didn't you?"

"You are much braver than I," Aunt Em said. "I should not like to stay at the Dog & Duck. People who spend nights there have a rather unfortunate habit of getting themselves killed."

Milly laughed out loud.

Em peered towards the door. "Who have you left lingering in the hallway?"

"My sister." Evelyn's lips twitched. "She's going to be staying with us for a while. I hope you don't mind."

"I suppose that child belongs to her?" Aunt Em pointed out of the window to where James was making snow angels.

"That is James, he is the middle child." Evelyn exchanged a look with Milly. "His elder sister, Leah, is very quiet and well behaved."

"I rather like naughty little boys who are full of spirit."

"In that case, you will absolutely adore James, Lady Emily."

"I will take Leah and Samuel with me to find Mrs Chapman." Evelyn waved a hand at her sister, when Milly moved to follow her sister. "You are supposed to be resting. So sit and rest, talk to Aunt Em and I shall go organise things for a change."

**

Not long afterwards, Evelyn was on her way back to the village with a fully stocked hamper and a small suitcase for herself and Tommy. Davey sat on the floor of the carriage, his tail thumping noisily with excitement.

Evelyn had only visited the nursery floor once in the five months she had lived at Hessleham Hall. In the early days, she had explored every room of her new home, and still remained amazed how many of them seemed to serve no purpose at all.

Upon hearing the news that there would be guests at the manor, Mrs Chapman began organising the work that needed doing with her usual efficiency. As Evelyn left, beds were being aired, one of the maids was checking all the toys in the playroom, another was mopping what already looked to Evelyn to be a very clean floor.

Mrs O'Connell was ordering Nora about in the kitchen. Not only did she want to make a special dinner for the guests, she had already ordered

Partridge to return shortly before dinner so she was able to send food back into the village for them both.

Evelyn smiled as she remembered Mrs O'Connell telling Partridge that she was making Lord Northmoor's favourite, jam roly poly pudding and as she was aware he was also partial to that particular dessert, he had jolly well better ride back to the manor that evening and she would make sure he had an extra helping.

Her mind full of Milly's advice and plans that were starting to form of things she could do to help those less fortunate than herself, they were soon back at the village.

Partridge helped her down from the carriage but, as he did so, Evelyn dropped Davey's lead. The puppy took full advantage of his freedom and an entire village of new and unusual scents and took off down the lane.

"My Lady, go inside, I shall chase Davey down."

"He is more likely to come back for me than you," Evelyn said. "I'll go after him, you take our luggage in. I shall be back in no time at all."

She hurried off in the direction Davey had taken. He really should be out of this habit of running off by now. Evelyn could not remember Nancy ever being as disobedient as Davey was.

A flash of black fur stood out against the white of the snow and indicated that Davey had detoured down a garden path. It looked as though he had headed towards Isolde's house. That did not surprise Evelyn, she had visited her friend with Davey many times in the past and Isolde often spoilt the dog with treats.

Davey ran across the lawn and into the back garden. Evelyn had a moment to think of how unusual it was for the gate to be standing open when Davey began barking and scratching at the

132

coal bunker. Quite certain the puppy had found a mouse, or some other small animal Evelyn had no wish to meet, she stood back and prepared to catch him when he got bored of his quarry.

Suddenly the breath was knocked out of her as something slammed hard into her back. Laying on her front, with her face in the snow, Evelyn quickly realised that someone was kneeling on her back. She tried to push herself up, but she was no match for whoever was on top of her.

The pressure eased slightly and Evelyn breathed a sigh of relief, thinking whoever it was had simply slid on ice and knocked her over by accident. However, her respite was short lived as a piece of soft material was hooked underneath her chin. It took her only a moment to be certain the red wool of a scarf had not been placed there to keep her warm.

Evelyn gasped as the pressure was increased.

She was being strangled!

Struggling, she fought to force her fingers underneath the scarf but she couldn't reduce the compression on her neck. She tried to gasp, but she couldn't catch her breath.

All she could do was thrash her legs about and hope that she managed to kick her assailant and knock him off balance. Her attempts were futile and her vision began to swim. Dimly she was aware of Davey still barking. Surely the din he was making would bring someone to her rescue.

As suddenly as the attack started, it stopped. Evelyn couldn't move, she lay panting on the ground. Tears stung at the back of her eyes, and she blinked them away, wanting to check she was definitely in Isolde's garden and not floating off up to heaven.

"My Lady, My Lady!" Partridge screamed as he turned her over onto her back. "Can you hear me?"

"Quite well, Partridge, my ears have not been boxed." Her voice sounded dreadful, just as Elsie Warren's had. Raspy and scratchy as though she were forcing words past a dry throat.

Davey chose that moment to stop barking and came over to lick Evelyn's face thoroughly. She pushed the ground behind her to try and sit up.

Partridge held a hand on one of her shoulders and with Davey's head next to her she was as effectively pinned to the ground as she had been moment earlier.

"Stay still, My Lady, I need to fetch the doctor. You shouldn't move." Partridge's eyes were wide with fear.

"I haven't fallen over," Evelyn said patiently. "I don't have any injuries that necessitate me staying still. I have, however, been horribly assaulted and would rather like to get off this freezing ground and to somewhere warm."

"Yes, of course, sorry." He helped Evelyn to her feet, caught hold of Davey's lead and put a steadying arm around her shoulders.

"Before we go anywhere, check that coal bunker."

"Whoever attacked you escaped over the fence, I am afraid." Partridge pointed to the wooden structure at the end of Isolde's garden. "I should have chased him. I would've caught him. I know I would."

"Did you see who it was?"

Partridge shook his head. "I grabbed him, and he took off immediately. He did leave this behind, though."

"A red woollen scarf." Evelyn glanced at the item in dismay. "I think everyone in Hessleham owns a garment exactly like that. I've lost count of the amount of people I have seen with one the last couple of days. Now, please, check what is in that structure!"

Her voice wavered at the end of her sentence and she was aware she sounded a little hysterical. Partridge gave her a look that left her in no doubt he thought she had taken leave of her senses, but he went over and lifted the lid.

"Coal, My Lady," he said as he turned back to her.

"Rummage around a bit, man!" she returned sharply.

Partridge did as she ordered and she heard him gasp before he faced her again. "There's a knife in here. One of those thin bladed ones that doctors use."

"Don't touch it," she warned. "Have you got a handkerchief?"

"Yes, should I use that to pick it up?"

"Be careful not to get your fingerprints on it." Evelyn coughed, she really needed to get in out of the cold and put clean dry clothes on.

Partridge pulled the weapon out from amongst the coal and brought it over to Evelyn.

"You're right, it's a scalpel," she said. "Like you would expect a doctor to have in his medical bag."

"Lord Northmoor will know what to do with it," Partridge said confidently. "Shall I help you or are you able to manage?"

Evelyn indicated his hands. He held the thin bladed knife in one and Davey's lead in the other. "I rather think you have your hands full."

Chapter Thirteen

Davey pulled so hard on his lead when he saw Tommy inside the pub that Partridge let him go.

"I shouldn't admit this when you're such a little rascal, but I have missed you." Tommy petted Davey and accepted a lick to the chin.

"Um…My Lord…" Partridge stammered, holding out the scalpel. "There has been a development."

Tommy looked at Evelyn. "Did Davey find this?"

"He did."

"Oh, you are a clever fellow." Tommy scratched the exact spot under Davey's ears that he loved. The dog wriggled in ecstasy. "I told your mistress you could do it, but she didn't believe me."

"Thomas Christie!" Evelyn admonished. "It is all very well giving that animal all of your affection for a job well done, but you have yet to notice that I have been the victim of a brutal attack."

Tommy looked between Evelyn and Partridge. Finally he noticed his wife's hair was no longer neatly pinned in place and the long dark locks had fallen about her shoulders.

He rushed to her side "Darling?"

"I am perfectly fine, thanks to Partridge."

"Partridge?"

"It was the dog, really. He barked his head off. Led me straight to Lady Northmoor."

"And?" Tommy shouted the word in utter frustration.

"A chap was on top of Lady Northmoor…"

"I shall kill him." Tommy pulled Evelyn into an embrace as though the attacker had come back, and he needed to protect her that very moment.

She pushed him away. "Calm down, you can see I have not been greatly harmed. Let Partridge finish the story."

"Do you need a brandy for your nerves?"

Evelyn sighed. "Tommy, if you need a brandy for *your* nerves, please just get one. And don't forget to mark it on the list George keeps behind the bar."

Tommy stared at Evelyn to reassure himself that she had suffered no lasting ill effects. Finally, he crossed over to the bar. "Shall we all have a drink?"

Partridge held out the knife again. "I should like to do something with this."

"Of course." Tommy took the weapon from his estate manager and wondered what on earth he was supposed to do with crucial evidence? Where could he put it so it would be safe until the police arrived?

"I am going to check on Leonard Williams." Partridge moved towards the door to the upstairs of the pub.

Tommy put out a hand. "Why are you checking on him? He was fine when you took his breakfast to him this morning, wasn't he? I haven't heard a peep out of him while you have been gone."

"Tommy, darling." Evelyn walked over to her husband and put her arms around his waist. "Let Partridge check on Len. Get your drink and come and sit down."

He kissed the top of her head. "I should be the one taking care of you."

"Once you calm down, I am certain you will do exactly that."

Tommy held her at arm's length so he could properly look her over. Scratches and bruises were blooming on the slender column of her neck. He reached out and touched her pale skin. "Does it hurt?"

"It's unpleasant, but I am feeling better."

"We shall have Teddy give you a thorough examination," Tommy said, indicating the doctor who was sitting at a table in the pub's corner.

In the commotion when she returned with Partridge and Davey, he didn't think she had even noticed Teddy and Isolde sitting quietly with their hands firmly joined.

"I shall have a gin and tonic," Evelyn said. "Heavy on the gin, light on the tonic."

"Teddy, Isolde?" Tommy asked. "Will either of you join us?"

They both shook their heads as Partridge came back downstairs. "If I may, My Lord, I would very much appreciate a brandy. Our prisoner has not escaped."

"Absolutely." Tommy slapped him on the back. "You have saved the day, as I understand it."

"Not exactly, My Lord." Partridge grimaced. "In fact, you may well be quite cross with me when you hear the full story."

"Nonsense." Evelyn patted one of the vacant chairs. "Come and sit here with us."

"I couldn't, My Lady, it wouldn't be at all proper."

"Stand behind me, if you would prefer, but come over here near me, please." Evelyn rubbed her throat. "My voice isn't its usual robust self, and we have a story to tell."

Tommy smiled as he prepared the drinks. Evelyn's voice was never hearty, but her words had

138

the effect she desired as Partridge took his healthy measure of brandy from Tommy and moved to stand directly behind her.

"Do carry on now, Partridge," Evelyn encouraged as Tommy sat next to her and placed their drinks on the table in front of them.

Partridge cleared his throat. "As I said, a man was on top of Lady Northmoor, and he had a scarf wrapped around her neck. I could see immediately he was pulling it tight and depriving Lady Northmoor of air."

Tommy was glad his back was to his estate manager. Although this was a far from amusing tale, the fastidious tone Partridge was using was so unlike his usual jovial speech as to sound slightly ridiculous.

"It was tied rather severely," Evelyn agreed.

"Where did this awful incident happen?" Isolde asked.

"On your rear lawn!" Evelyn turned to her friend. "I was laying there having the life squeezed out of me while Davey was barking loud enough to raise the dead. I wondered why you didn't hear him, open your door, and come to my aid."

"Teddy and I agreed last night that we should speak to you today." Isolde looked at Evelyn's injuries with sympathy. "I am so sorry that I was not home. I would certainly have taken a frying pan to the head of whoever was hurting you."

"That would have been very welcome." Evelyn turned to smile at Partridge. "Fortunately, I had my very own hero who came to my rescue."

"I dealt the rogue a blow to the side of his head which knocked him to the ground," Partridge went on. "I immediately checked on Lady Northmoor."

"Which was the correct thing to do," Evelyn reassured him.

"I do regret, My Lord." Partridge looked earnestly at Tommy. "That I did not chase after the assailant."

"My wife is correct," Tommy soothed. "I would have been most disconcerted if you had left Lady Northmoor injured in the snow. I still don't understand how this happened."

"Ah, well, that is where Davey did not cover himself with glory, I am afraid." Evelyn grimaced.

"How so?"

"When Partridge helped me down from the carriage, he was so excited to be in the village that he pulled and I let go of his lead." Evelyn held up a hand. "Now, I know you will say Partridge should have chased Davey and I should have entered the safety of the pub. However, I thought he would be more likely to respond to me. He ran into Isolde's garden, and the rest you know."

"Where was the knife found?"

"In the coal bunker in Mrs Newley's garden," Partridge answered. "The dog was barking at it and completely ignored the attack on Lady Northmoor."

"So I deduced there was something in there more important to Davey than my physical health." Evelyn smiled wryly. "Perhaps you could take a look at it, Teddy?"

Dr Mainwaring let go of Isolde's hand and walked over to the bar where Tommy had placed the bloodstained implement. He peered closely at it, but did not move it from where it rested on Partridge's handkerchief.

"It is certainly sharp enough to do the damage Reg spoke of."

"One of yours?" Evelyn asked.

"Evelyn!" Isolde exclaimed. "Oh, please, let us not do this again. You cannot believe Teddy would do such a thing."

"Isolde, dear," Evelyn mollified the other woman. "I do not mean it as an accusation against Teddy, only if the knife belonged to him."

"I have one similar." Teddy nodded. "I will check my bag and see if mine is there or if this is it."

"May I ask a bold question?" Tommy asked. "As you said when you arrived here this morning that you had something specific to tell us, now might be a good time for us to ask you some further questions."

"If you do not need me anymore, My Lord, I should let you talk privately to your friends." He looked around the room. "Where are Elsie and Mrs Warren?"

"They went to wait at Reg's house when Teddy and Isolde arrived," Tommy explained.

"The luggage is just inside the door. Should I bring it inside before I leave? I brought it down off the carriage, then abandoned it to look for Lady Northmoor."

Tommy stood and shook Partridge's hand. "You have done more than enough, my man. You can expect a token of my heartfelt appreciation when we are back at the manor."

"Oh, My Lord, no. I cannot accept a payment for doing what any man would have done in my position."

"Never turn down a gift before you know what it is," Evelyn advised with a smile.

"I am much obliged, Lord Northmoor."

As soon as Partridge left, and Teddy had retaken his seat, Isolde raised an eyebrow at Tommy. "Your bold question?"

"I think I should like to ask one first," Evelyn put in. "We have been told in the course of our investigations that Teddy was involved in a verbal disagreement with Phillip Newley on Friday evening. The time in question was immediately prior to closing time. Is that correct?"

Although Evelyn looked at Teddy, it was Isolde who answered. "That is absolute nonsense. Teddy was with me Friday evening. That is why we came to see you this morning. We are together most evenings."

"Is that so?"

"Evelyn, I am more than well aware that you were observant enough to see Teddy's slippers underneath the chair in the parlour."

"The footprints in the snow leading to the back of the house really gave away the fact someone had visited your house and, that person did not want to stand on the front doorstep where they may be seen." Tommy looked at Teddy. "Though, of course, they could have been left by whoever dropped the knife in Isolde's coal bunker."

Teddy squared his shoulders. "They are mine."

"Now we know what we are telling you makes us look very immoral." Isolde looked sadly at Evelyn. "And Teddy and I have not been entirely honest with you by pretending we have been able to remain friends."

"We simply couldn't," Teddy added. "The depth of our love has just been enormously overwhelming."

"Can you forgive us?" Isolde pleaded.

"It is not for Tommy and I to give forgiveness."

"We spoke to John first thing this morning. We have also prayed about this a great deal. What we have done is a great sin."

"I would imagine the vicar will find your situation easier to reconcile if you are to make things official." Tommy looked pointedly at the ring that now sat on Isolde's finger rather than on a chain around her neck.

"He will marry us as soon as it is decent." Isolde blushed. "I know it may well be frowned upon for me to wear Teddy's ring so swiftly."

"There will be talk around the village about rushing down the aisle." Evelyn laughed. "They will prepare to do their maths!"

Teddy reached over and put a hand over Isolde's. "I am afraid that, on this occasion, the gossip would be accurate."

Tommy caught the look of pain that flashed across Evelyn's face before she jumped to her feet. "Tommy, Teddy and Isolde do not have a drink. We must toast them on their new engagement and on their joyous news."

He watched his wife busy herself behind the bar getting drinks for their friends and knew that, despite the cheerful air she projected, internally she was hurting once more.

***

Evelyn shared in her friends' joy for as long as she was able before excusing herself by saying she needed to change her clothes.

Tommy had carried up the suitcase she had packed for them back at the manor. It seemed like an age since she had been in her warm, safe house watching her nephews and niece enjoy the things she took for granted.

She had told Tommy to go back downstairs with their friends as she needed a few moments to herself. Although she had been relaxed about the attack on her life, it had shaken her to her very core.

After she had washed, put on clean, dry clothes and pinned her hair back up, Evelyn sat at the dresser and regarded herself in the mirror. Who would do such a thing to her?

She tried to go through the things they had learned the previous afternoon. It was obvious that something someone had told them was the key to the entire business. The murderer had become afraid that she and Tommy were getting close to solving the mystery.

If that assumption was correct, it made it highly likely that whoever it was would not stop now they had become so desperate as to attack her in broad daylight.

Evelyn turned the collar of her up to hide the marks on her neck, but then a thought occurred to her. Tommy knocked on the door to the room and she called out for him to come in.

"Do you think George would let me borrow his red scarf?"

"What on earth for?"

Evelyn tipped her head. "It would hide these marks on my neck. But, also, imagine the murderer's face when they see me both alive and well but wearing a garment similar to the one they used to try and end my life."

"That's a very dangerous game to play." Tommy shook his head. "I cannot allow it."

"I know you are jolly afraid because of what happened," she said sympathetically. "But we must not let that impede our investigation."

He thought for a moment. "No."

"Tommy," she cajoled. "Since when have you been able to tell me what I can or cannot wear?"

It was a low blow, but one she felt the need to make for the good of their investigation.

"I don't like it." He stared at her with sorrow in his eyes. "It's akin to goading the person into making another attempt on your life."

"As I am sure you will not leave my side any time soon, I should think I will be quite safe." Evelyn eyed the bloody scalpel in his hands. "Now, please put that thing somewhere safe, seeing it is making me quite queasy."

Tommy reached up and put it on top of the wardrobe. "Shall we check Newley's room now before we go back out to continue our questioning?"

"Goodness, you are clever to remember that, I completely forgot."

They moved out into the hallway. Tommy locked the door, checked that it was secure and put the key into his right-hand trouser pocket. From the other pocket, he extracted another key.

He put it into the door marked with a number three, and they went inside. Clothes were strewn haphazardly across the room, the bed was unmade, and the dressing table was littered with toiletries.

"Not a very fastidious fellow," Tommy commented.

"The very opposite," Evelyn agreed. "Do you think someone has already been through his room?"

He shook his head and pointed to a partially open drawer. "Doubtful, there's a bundle of notes in there."

"Unless they were looking for something else in there and not money."

"Possibly." He held up a sheaf of papers. "See here? These are the release documents in relation to his last incarceration."

"Bring those with us," Evelyn decided. "If Violet Rogers wants any proof that her fiancé was a dishonest man, those are the documents we may require."

"There doesn't seem to be anything personal in here at all." Tommy opened drawers and quickly sifted through the contents.

"Did he have a wallet on him when he died?"

"Goodness, I didn't think to get Reg to check. How careless of me."

Evelyn moved back to the door. "We shall add that to our list of things to do today. Should we speak to everyone again? I am keen to move things along. There doesn't appear to be anything here that will help us."

"I agree, let us go to the vicarage first as I believe we have a few questions for John and we need to check the veracity of Percy's story with Hilda."

Evelyn snorted. "If we can get her to answer the door!"

Chapter Fourteen

They walked the short distance towards the vicarage with Evelyn sporting George's scarf around her neck. They stopped at Isolde's house to check if the red scarf was still lying on the lawn in her rear garden.

Evelyn trembled as she surveyed the scene of her attack. Tommy picked up the scarf by spearing it with a knitting needle he had borrowed from Mrs Hughes. He deposited it into a paper bag.

"There now, darling." Tommy tucked Evelyn close to his side. "We will keep this safe until the police can get here. I'm not sure there's anything at all that they can do with it. Certainly, they cannot lift fingerprints from wool, but we should keep it safe. It is evidence."

Evelyn shivered. "I wish we had brought Davey. Though I think today has showed that he is of absolutely no use as a guard dog."

"Let's get you away from here." He looked at her in concern. "Are you sure you wish to continue today? Perhaps you could stay with Isolde or I will have Partridge take you back to the manor?"

"The poor man has already made the journey twice and Cook is insistent he goes back before dinner and brings our meals back with him."

"They will be cold." Tommy frowned in confusion.

"She seems to think she has a way to keep them warm that involves hot plates, warmed bricks and a particularly fast moving carriage."

"Hmm. Ordinarily I would not distrust Cook's word but on this occasion I think she might be wrong."

"I promise I will never again resent dressing for dinner and sitting at our table for a warm meal." Evelyn lay her head against Tommy's shoulder. "Please let's go to the vicarage now."

"Of course." Tommy led them back onto the path, and they walked down to the vicarage. He rapped on the door knocker. "I wonder how long it will take her to answer this time."

Evelyn tried to keep her teeth from chattering as they stood waiting. The sun had made an appearance, though it was far from warm, it had begun the slow process of melting the snow. However, Evelyn was now shaking not because of the temperature, but because she had returned to the place she had been attacked and it had made her realise how very lucky had been.

The door opened to reveal John. He wore a bulky cardigan over his shirt and trousers. "How delightful, the Northmoors!"

"Where is that woman?" Tommy asked, agitation obvious in his voice.

"Probably in the kitchen." John looked positively taken aback at his friend's tone.

"I am sorting this issue of yours out immediately." Tommy marched down the hallway. "Please look after Evelyn, she has had a very difficult morning."

He pushed open the kitchen door to find Hilda asleep in front of a roaring fire with her mouth hanging open. Tommy picked up a frying pan that looked as though it contained the remnants of the eggs she had served for breakfast that morning. Grabbing a wooden spoon from next to the sink, he banged it loudly onto the bottom of the pan.

Hilda jumped to her feet. Her face darkened to puce, and she opened her mouth, eyes flashing angrily. She seemed to think better of whatever it was she was going to say and closed her mouth.

"Lord Northmoor," she said stiffly.

"What, may I ask, is going on in this house?"

Hilda eyed him warily. "What do you mean?"

"Your job, as I believe it to be, is a housemaid?"

Her chin raised a notch. "Yes."

"And those duties cover such things as preparing the vicar's meals, answering his door, the telephone, laundry and general cleaning as required. Is that correct?"

"Yes, My Lord."

Tommy swiped a finger across the sideboard and then looked at the accumulated dust in disgust. "It seems to me the only room you keep passably clean is the parlour because that is the one you know guests will see. Is the rest of the house kept as slovenly as this one?"

Hilda's lips pursed as though to deny his suggestion, but Tommy saw the moment she told the truth. "It is too big a job for me, My Lord. I suffer terribly with my nerves."

Tommy thought of George Hughes and an angry retort formed. He bit it back as he remembered where he was. The very least he could do was an attempt a Christian response. "I am very sorry to hear that. Perhaps the parish could find you a less demanding job of work?"

"But what about the vicar?"

She was probably more worried about a drop in her wages if she took a less demanding job. "I am certain we will be able to find a replacement for you if you genuinely find this work too much for you."

"Well…maybe…"

"Perhaps your sister, who I believe you visited last year when she was ill, knows of something near where she lives? I expect she would be glad of your company."

Hilda could hardly backtrack on what she had already said about her nerves, now the reality of leaving the easy life she had made for herself in the vicarage was staring her in the face.

"I shall write and ask her."

"Good, that is settled then." Tommy smiled agreeably. "I will see if the parish knows of someone who could take over your duties. I will write a letter. Perhaps you will let the vicar know when you expect to settle with your sister?"

Hilda nodded balefully, as though she wasn't quite sure how this had happened. "Yes, My Lord."

"Now, I wonder if you can cast your mind back to yesterday morning? Specifically, I would like to know if there may have been a knock on the door at around the time the vicar came home for blankets?"

"Weeeelllll," Hilda stretched the word out for at least five syllables. "There may have been."

"Might you have been having a morning snooze?"

"It is possible."

Tommy looked at the bells on the wall that should warn Hilda when the bell was pulled in the parlour, or someone was at the front door. "Goodness. It looks as though the ropes are frayed. I wonder, perhaps, if there are mice in the kitchen because of the unclean conditions?"

"Well, really, I do not have mice in my kitchen!" Hilda bellowed, completely outraged.

"What other explanation do you have for ropes on each of the bells that you should be able to hear, and answer, being damaged? If it is not mice…" Tommy shrugged, leaving the insinuation hanging that if rodents had not caused the destruction, then it must be deliberate damage.

"You may well be lord of the manor, but I do not have to listen to you speaking to me in this manner."

"You most certainly do not," Tommy agreed affably.

"I think I shall telephone to my sister." Hilda moved towards the hallway.

"I think that is a very wise decision." Tommy followed her, aware Hilda was waiting for him to tell her that a telephone call wouldn't be necessary. "I shall be in the parlour with the vicar and my wife. Please let us know your decision forthwith."

Tommy marched back down the corridor and into the parlour.

Evelyn looked at his face. "Tommy, what have you done?"

"It isn't what I've done." He pointed in the direction of the back of the house. "It is what that idle woman has *not* done."

"Tommy!" Evelyn pierced him with her most strict look. "What has happened?"

He looked apologetically at John. "I rather think I have left you with no help at all after today."

Tommy looked around the parlour. The grate hadn't been swept that morning, the coal bucket sitting next to the fire was empty, and it didn't look as though Hilda had even thought about preparing a morning tea tray let alone begun doing so. To his mind, losing John's maid was not a problem but a blessing.

"Oh dear," John said. "Where will she go?"

"She is telephoning to her sister as we speak."

"Come and stay with us at the manor until we sort out a replacement for you," Evelyn suggested.

"Shall we have the entire village to stay?" Tommy enquired with a laugh.

"Perhaps if you didn't scare his staff away, Tommy, the vicar wouldn't be in this predicament."

Tommy held out his hands in front of him, his face a mask of innocence. "She decided herself."

"I apologise for my husband." Evelyn turned to the vicar. "We have something to ask you about yesterday morning."

"Of course, how can I help?"

"When you left the church to get blankets, did you see anyone else?"

John shook his head. "I did not, who else would I have seen? Everyone else was either in church or their own homes."

"Percy Armstrong said he came to the vicarage to ask Hilda to make tea for Mrs Rogers."

"He may well have done." John looked helplessly between Evelyn and Tommy. "I went upstairs to the laundry cupboard and he could have called then. It's also possible he went directly to the back door. A lot of villagers do, you know, because they know it's more likely that door will be answered."

"So you didn't see him, but that doesn't mean he didn't come here, as he said?"

"Percy is a frequent visitor to the vicarage. He would be well aware the back door would be the quickest route to getting a cup of tea."

"Thank you, vicar." Tommy got to his feet and opened the door. Hilda stood on the other side.

The woman ignored Tommy and addressed the vicar. "My sister has asked me to stay with her indefinitely. As you know, I would never leave you in the lurch, but she has an immediate need."

"Of course, if you must go, I shall be sorry to see you go." John walked over to his desk and pulled out the chair. "I will write a letter of reference while you pack your things."

Hilda put a hand up to her mouth to stifle a cry and fled from the room.

"I think you were supposed to put up at least a token argument." Evelyn laughed. "Please don't let her change your mind about her staying before the buses run again."

***

They walked back down the lane, stopping at the pub so Tommy could put the scarf that had been used to strangle Evelyn on the top of the wardrobe with the knife.

"Alfred Cross next," Tommy said. "We must get the truth out of him today, and I think I know exactly how to do it."

Evelyn wrinkled her nose. "Is this going to be one of those times when you do something I don't very much like?"

"Possibly," Tommy admitted. "But you must understand, darling, after what happened to you I am even more keen to get this matter resolved. I will do whatever it takes to do that."

When Alfred answered the door, he frowned. "What more can you possibly want? You were untruthful yesterday and your wife upset my sister."

"Your sister was dreadfully upset, Mr Cross, because her fiancé was killed yesterday morning."

"Fiancé?" Alfred repeated. "Whatever do you mean?"

"Goodness," Evelyn said, her voice dripping with sugary sweetness. "Have I said something I shouldn't have? Were you not aware that your sister was engaged to Mr Newley?"

"It's true, Alfred," Violet said as she came up the corridor to stand behind her brother. "I think we should take this conversation off the doorstep. It isn't something I want the village to be gossiping about for months to come."

Alfred led them into the parlour. He stood back and allowed the ladies to take the only two seats in the small room.

"I shall get straight to the point," Tommy said. "I don't want to make this any harder for either of you than it already is."

"What a lovely scarf, Lady Northmoor," Violet remarked. "My brother has one just like it. I believe Miss Armstrong knitted it for him."

Alfred flushed. "I think perhaps she was keen on me at one point."

Evelyn tried to remember how many people she had seen with a red scarf over the last twenty-four hours, and if they were all men who Ellen had hoped would be so grateful for the small gift, they would take her away from the difficult life she seemed to live with her brother.

"She's a very lovely young woman," Evelyn said. "Whoever she marries will be an exceedingly lucky man."

"She's not for me," Alfred retorted. "Her brother is very odd."

"He seems very intense," Tommy said. "Now, Mr Cross, the question I want to ask you today comes because of other information we have received. It is my understanding that you and Mr Williams had an arrangement where you covered for each other in the event one of you wished to leave the church for any reason."

"Why would I want to leave the church?" Alfred frowned in disdain at Tommy. "I go to church for the service, not to avoid it."

"Sorry, I should have made myself clearer," Tommy said. "You cover for Mr Williams when he leaves the church, and because of that he covers for you when you take money out of the collection plate."

"How dare you!" Alfred shouted. "How dare you insult me in that way in my own house?"

"Perhaps you would share with us what your second job is?" Evelyn asked.

"What second job? Have you gone as batty as your husband?"

"That is enough!" Tommy thundered. "Apologise to my wife at once and answer the question. Otherwise, I am more than happy to harness my horse to the plough and clear the road all the way to York and deposit you at the police station myself."

"I apologise, Lady Northmoor." Alfred barely looked at Evelyn as he delivered the words in an exceedingly sulky voice. "I don't have a second job."

"But, Alfred." Violet shook her head in disbelief. "I've already told Lady Northmoor that you have another job. You must have because you keep giving me little extras for the kiddies."

"Leonard pays for my silence," Alfred said sulkily.

"I apologise, Mrs Rogers, but would you mind leaving us whilst we discuss something highly confidential with your brother?"

Violet looked only too happy to leave the room. She put a hand on her brother's shoulder as she passed by him. "What have you done, Alfred? Just what have you done?"

"Go see to the children, Vi, I will sort this out."

Once the door closed behind Violet Rogers, Tommy turned back to Alfred. "I think we both know the few coins Len threw your way for your silence did not add up to the money you needed to care for your sister and her children."

"The vicar always emphasised the money was to go to the poor and needy," Alfred muttered, looking at his shoes. "There was no one more destitute than Vi when she came to live with me."

"But you didn't realise how much money three extra mouths and the things the children needed would cost you?"

Alfred shook his head miserably. "I took a little at first. Just for food. But there was always something extra they needed. And Vi didn't qualify for state help because Harold tried to run away when he was in France."

"Then he was shot as a deserter?" Tommy asked in dismay.

Alfred put a hand up to his forehead. "I couldn't even fight. Flat feet. I tried to get Harold to say he was me so he could stay home with Vi and the children, but he refused."

"So you felt it was your duty to support your sister and her children?" Evelyn asked sympathetically.

"Yes, but I couldn't make ends meet."

"To be clear." Tommy waited until Alfred looked up and met his gaze. "You have been taking money out of the collection plate, and it was not Phillip Newley?"

"As I said, I took a few coins," Alfred explained. "Len saw me and then got me to cover for him while he canoodled with Elsie Warren. And then…"

"Yes?" Tommy wanted to shake the answers out of Alfred so they could find out the truth and then confront the person who was to blame for the murder of Phillip Newley and the attack on Evelyn.

"Then Mr Newley somehow knew what I was doing and told me to take more money otherwise he would let the entire village know what a harlot my sister was." Alfred's cheeks flushed red and he looked thoroughly dejected. "Violet has already been through so much, but Newley claimed their relationship was much advanced and if she was to become pregnant, then everyone would know her shame."

"There's something more you're not telling," Tommy pressed. "I know there's more."

"No, no, there isn't My Lord. Is that not enough? I am a common thief, and my sister has been having relations with a man who is not her husband. How could our lives be any sorrier?"

It was hard to argue with Alfred's logic, and despite his deep desire to shake the truth out of the man, Tommy accepted they would not get any further than they already had.

Chapter Fifteen

"Did you believe him?" Tommy asked Evelyn as they walked back down the lane towards the village post office and another meeting with Percy Armstrong and his sister.

"I thought he was afraid."

"Yes, I did too. But what of?"

"I think it's a who. He is afraid of someone."

"The person who killed Phillip Newley?"

"Yes," Evelyn said. "I think he knows exactly who it is, and he's keeping that person's identity a secret because he is terrified of being handed the same fate as Newley."

"This is rather stating the obvious, but if we do not resolve this quickly, there is going to be another murder."

Once again, Percy saw them approach through the shop window and moved to let them in. He stared at the scarf around Evelyn's neck as he let them through. "That looks like one of Ellen's creations."

"Oh, do you think so?" Evelyn forced a smile onto her frozen lips.

"She has made many similar." Percy laughed. "She makes them when she becomes infatuated with a man. Once they resist her rather futile attempts at conversation, she makes another and transfers her affection. I find it rather odd she has given a gift such as that to a woman."

"Do you have a scarf like that?" Tommy asked.

"I do not, I am her brother."

"Of course," Tommy nodded as though he agreed with Percy. "You have just explained she only makes them for people she likes."

Percy looked confused, then seemed to decide Tommy had suggested nothing offensive. "Would you like to go upstairs?"

"I think I do. I'd rather like to see your charming sister again." Tommy smiled affably. "Perhaps she will have some strawberry jam I can buy from her. We are nearly completely out of the supplies I bought at the fete last year."

Percy lifted the end of the counter so they could move out of the shop area and towards the stairs that would take them to his private quarters. He called out as he climbed the steps. "We have visitors, sister!"

Ellen came to the top of the staircase, then disappeared again. Percy led them into a beautifully decorated parlour with a small table against the back wall. On the table was a white cloth that had been delicately embroidered with yellow roses. Evelyn walked over for a closer look.

"What exquisite work. Where did you get this, Ellen?"

"I made it, My Lady."

"Goodness, what a talent," Evelyn praised. "You should sell these downstairs and at the fete. Do you make clothes too?"

"I make my own," Ellen replied shyly.

"You should open a shop," Evelyn advised. "Fashion is transforming these days. You would have a never ending supply of work from the ladies in the village. Especially when everyone seems so busy these days they don't have time for their own mending."

"I don't have the time for that." Ellen looked towards Percy. "I help Percy in the shop and do the accounts for the business. I make things in my spare time but could never do it professionally."

"You certainly couldn't," Percy agreed. "The time you spend messing around with fripperies could be better spent dusting shelves downstairs or rearranging displays."

If Ellen's 'fripperies' were what decorated the room they were in, Evelyn thought the woman had a talent that her brother was woefully underestimating.

"We shall talk later," Evelyn said, smiling brightly at Ellen.

"I'm afraid I have a few problems with what you both told me yesterday," Tommy said, injected a note of sadness into his voice. "So I must go through some of those things again."

"Of course, My Lord," Percy simpered, so eager to please and ingratiatingly polite when he addressed Tommy, which was in complete contrast to the demeaning way he often spoke to his sister. "What can we do for you?"

Evelyn put a hand up to her forehead. "Oh dear, I feel rather faint suddenly."

"Goodness, darling." Tommy hooked an arm around Evelyn and helped her over to a chair.

"Do not mention Teddy and Isolde and what they spoke to us about," she whispered as he leaned over her.

"Do you think we may have some tea?" Tommy looked at Ellen. "Hot and sweet if you don't mind?"

"Of course, Lord Northmoor." Ellen hurried off.

"What is wrong with her?" Percy enquired.

"I am quite alright," Evelyn said shakily. "Do carry on your conversation, Tommy."

Evelyn kept a tight hold of Tommy's hand.

"Can you let me know if you tried the front or the back door yesterday when you tried to get tea from the vicarage?"

"Any fool knows attempting to get an answer from the front of the house is mostly impossible," Percy said derisively. "I went directly to the rear of the house."

"And?"

"And there was no response," Percy simpered.

"Was that unusual?"

"I have just explained it was not."

"At the front, it was quite expected for Hilda to fail to answer. My understanding is that villagers tend to go to the back door because she answers that one."

"I see." Percy looked up as though considering his response. "She did not answer, and when I peered through the window, she was not anywhere in sight."

Ellen returned with a tea tray and poured a cup for Evelyn. "I hope this revives you, My Lady."

"That is very kind, thank you, Ellen." Evelyn put a hand over her teacup as Ellen moved the sugar bowl closer. "I know my husband said sweet, but I cannot abide sugar in my tea."

When they had all settled with their drinks, Tommy looked at Evelyn. "You look much better, darling. Is there anything you wanted to ask?"

"Not about the case." Evelyn effected a rather silly little laugh. "But perhaps you will indulge me asking Ellen another question about her needlework?"

Tommy patted her arm. "Always."

"Do you make wedding dresses?"

"I always planned on making my own." She looked away, as though seeing the dress she would've made for herself if she had been asked. "I have never made one for anyone else, but I am certain I could. Who is getting married?"

"Isolde Newley," Evelyn announced.

"Evelyn!" Tommy admonished. "What on earth has got into you?"

"Everyone will know they are to marry soon enough," she retorted.

"Mr Armstrong, Miss Armstrong." Tommy got to his feet. "I apologise most profusely on behalf of my wife. She is very clearly still feeling unwell. I must take her back to the Dog & Duck immediately."

"But Tommy," Evelyn protested. "Dr Mainwaring is to go to Isolde's house at two this afternoon to ask her the question officially."

"What are you doing?" he hissed into her ear as he tried to take the teacup out of Evelyn's hands and pull her to her feet.

Her only response was that ridiculous giggle that sounded nothing at all like Evelyn and something a child might think would get them out of trouble with their parents.

Percy stared at Evelyn in disgust. "Is she drunk?"

Tommy helped Evelyn to the stairs. "Can you get down safely?"

"Of course I can, I am not infirm."

"You are acting incredibly strangely."

"I shall explain outside," Evelyn whispered. "But do hurry, Tommy, we have no time to waste."

***

"Where are we going?"

"Immediately to Isolde's house."

He nodded. "You certainly need to apologise."

"Tommy, do we agree it appears as though someone is trying to frame Teddy?" she asked excitedly. "The red scarf which he wears, the scalpel, and the fact it was then found in Isolde's coal bunker."

"That would certainly fit some facts." Tommy ran a hand through his hair. "Are you are thinking the murderer is attempting to frame Teddy, and he then killed Phillip, because his ultimate prize is Isolde?"

"Yes," she murmured. "And if that is correct, don't you see that there is only person who it can be?"

"Not really."

"If it is someone that Alfred is afraid of, then it follows that this person arranged for Alfred to have his funny turn so he could leave church and commit the murder. Someone who was could promise Phillip Newley, a known blackmailer and lover of money, a small fortune if he divorced Isolde so he could have her for himself."

"We didn't find a sizeable amount of money in his room, remember?"

"He never paid the money." Evelyn grabbed Tommy's arm. "Why don't you see? He promised the money, arranged to pay it, then killed Phillip so he didn't have to pay it. Then he framed Teddy. Isolde is now free to marry and Teddy hangs for a murder he did not commit."

"I think I am beginning to see what you are saying."

***

Isolde crossed her living room and peeked through the curtains to her front door to see who was outside. Recognising a villager, she walked to her front door and unlocked it.

As soon as he was inside, he pushed her backwards into the parlour with alarming haste.

Isolde pressed herself against the high back of one of the chairs facing her fire. Other than the light thrown off by the coals, the room was in complete darkness.

"I am so glad you are now free and I can speak what is on my heart," he murmured into Isolde's ear. "My darling!"

"Goodness, this is unexpected." Isolde tried to wriggle away from his firm hold.

"You must know how I feel about you," he insisted. "I have done everything I can to free you from that awful husband of yours. All so we could be together."

"I don't know what to say."

"Say that you feel the love that I feel." He reached out and put a finger over her lips. "Or, at least, if you don't feel passionately about me at this moment, you have feelings that will grow."

"Of course, I like you very much."

He pressed his lips against hers. "I knew I was correct and you were dallying with the doctor to both make me jealous and to force your husband into divorcing you for adultery."

"Indeed," Isolde's voice was strained, but her pursuer did not seem to notice.

"I can buy you whatever you want. I am a very rich man," he boasted. "Where should you like to go on our honeymoon? I think a cruise then we can visit as many countries as you like."

"I will go wherever you would like to take me," Isolde replied. "But, please tell me, what happened to Phillip?"

"Do not be coy, darling!" He kissed her again. "I killed him so we could be together."

"I am quite speechless."

"Please, Isolde, my love." He put his lips against her throat and nuzzled her neck. "Let us go upstairs."

"I don't think so!" Evelyn stood on the cushion of the chair behind Isolde on which she had been hiding. She brandished a poker in her hand.

"I don't think so either!" Tommy snapped on the overhead light, and he and Teddy advanced on Percy Armstrong.

"But…but you can't be here!" he screamed.

"It was very simple." Tommy said grimly. "We stood behind the door. When you came in, all you had to do was turn around and you would've seen us, but you were concentrating only on Isolde."

"This cannot be happening." Percy slapped himself on the side of the head. "After all I have been through for you. I adore you. I have loved you from the very moment you came into the village. Isolde…please."

Isolde backed away from Percy and stood next to Evelyn. Her entire body trembled. Evelyn gripped one of her friend's hands. "You were utterly perfect."

"Bloody risky," Teddy said brusquely. He looked at Tommy. "I still don't know how you talked us into this."

"Let us get him back to the Dog & Duck and safely locked away until the police get here."

Tommy considered Percy. "The police aren't coming, are they?"

Percy's mouth twisted into a grotesque smile. "Not quite the stupid pretty boy I thought you were, are you, *Lord* Northmoor?"

"The person you underestimated was my wife," Tommy replied. "She was the one who worked out it was you."

"How did you know it was me?"

"When I visited your shop earlier today, I realised you are always in the front of your shop. You could easily have seen me return from the manor and took advantage of your chance to attack me. I don't really understand why though."

"To stop your meddling." Percy spat. "Long enough for me to finish the setup, then I would summon the police and give them the culprit together with the evidence."

"How would you do that?"

"I intended on filling Isolde's coal bucket for her and finding the knife. When I saw you go into her garden, I knew you had to be stopped."

Tommy forced his hands to relax. At that moment, he wanted nothing more than to wrap his hands around Percy Armstrong's neck and squeeze the air out of his lungs as he had done to Evelyn.

Teddy stepped forward. "Come on, old chap. Let's get this villain locked away somewhere safe and telegram for the police."

Tommy picked up the curtain tie Isolde had given him before Percy knocked on her door, and he used it to fasten Percy's hands securely in front of him.

The two men held one arm each and with Isolde and Evelyn following, they marched their prisoner back to the pub.

Mrs Hughes was downstairs behind the bar when they entered. "Heavens above!" she exclaimed. "Not another one."

Partridge stepped forward. "What shall I do with him, My Lord?"

Tommy pushed Percy forward. "This is the man who both killed Phillip Newley and attacked Lady Northmoor."

Partridge nodded grimly. "So lock him up and throw away the key?"

"I only wish that were possible," Tommy answered. "Can you go along to the post office and have Miss Armstrong send an urgent telegram to the police requesting their immediate assistance. Do not tell her that her brother is the person we have apprehended but bring her back with you so that I may speak to her and break the news."

"Shall we put him the cellar?" Mrs Hughes asked. "That poor girl does not need to be looking at her brother while you tell her the awful things he has been up to."

"Is there somewhere secure down there?"

"There is a secure room," she said. "George always said when people got too drunk he would throw them in there to sober up."

"Get that vile man out of my sight," Isolde said with feeling.

Mrs Hughes beckoned Tommy, and he followed her, keeping a tight hold on Percy as he did so.

Teddy moved to Isolde's side and wrapped his arms around her. "You are alright now, my sweetheart. I cannot wait to spend every day for the rest of my life loving you. I am the luckiest man alive."

"I'm so very glad my plan worked." Evelyn smiled at her friends.

"I was rather afraid you would get us all killed," Teddy admitted.

"You are going to be very busy," Isolde warned Evelyn. "I am going to need a lot of help from you in the next few months. I have a wedding to organise, I need a maid of honour, Teddy will require a best man, and then we will need godparents for our child. Who else would we ask but our very best friends?"

Evelyn's eyes stung with unshed tears but this time, not for what she wanted but didn't have, but with joy for her friends.

Chapter Sixteen

Aunt Em clapped her hands together, her eyes shining with excitement. "Sit down, hurry up, dears, we need to hear the entire story."

Evelyn and Tommy sat in the drawing room of Hessleham Manor, surrounded by their family and friends later that evening. Milly's children were in bed, being watched over by Elsie and her mother, which left Milly and Reg to enjoy an evening with adult company. Isolde and Teddy had also joined them for dinner.

"Where shall we start?" Evelyn teased.

"I don't mind where you start," Aunt Em replied tartly. "But do make sure you finish before the dinner gong goes. It isn't at all seemly to talk about murder over the dinner table."

Milly hid a laugh behind her hand.

Evelyn and Tommy regaled Aunt Em, Milly, and Reg with the story of the last twenty-four hours. It ended with the arrival of the police to take away Percy, Len, and Alfred Cross, together with the evidence that Tommy had recovered from the wardrobe in his room at the Dog & Duck.

"Wait." Aunt Em held up a hand. "I don't understand. You said the police could not get through because of the snow."

"Percy did not send a telegram. When he told me that the police had responded, he told me they could not get here because of the snow. He thought that would buy him a few more days to finish framing Dr Mainwaring."

"The devious little horror." Aunt Em shuddered. "And he half killed you. Are you certain you are quite recovered?"

"Yes, thank you, Aunt Em." Evelyn's smile felt a little wobbly despite her assurances. "However, I think I would like to have a nice long break from sleuthing if at all possible."

"I would suggest you don't go anywhere, and that will avoid murders falling into your laps." Aunt Em sipped her gin. "But the first two happened right here in the house and grounds."

"Maybe we should have a holiday," Tommy suggested.

"It does so happen that I have received a letter." Aunt Em plucked it from the table next to her. "It is from Aunt Victoria. She says she is returning to England and would like the use of our house in London. Perhaps you would like to accompany an old lady to the city?"

"That sounds a wonderful plan," Evelyn said.

"A nice, quiet family trip to London." Tommy nodded. "That is a champion idea, Aunt Em."

"The only murder and madness we will encounter will be on the stage, I am sure."

"Are you certain you wouldn't be bored?" Aunt Em asked.

"Positively." Evelyn finished her drink. "I am quite finished with murder."

THE END

MURDER IN BELGRAVE SQUARE
COMING 30th APRIL 2021

Tommy & Evelyn Christie were hoping for a break from solving murders when they agreed to host Aunt Victoria and her daughters, Madeleine and Elise at their London home in Belgrave Square.

Recently widowed Victoria has returned from France for the London Season and to mend bridges with her estranged family.

None of them were prepared for the doubly shocking sight of a newborn baby and a dead body on the back doorstep of their imposing London residence.

Tommy & Evelyn face a race against time to solve the murder and the mystery of the abandoned baby before cousin Madeleine's London Season is ruined.

A Note from Catherine

Thank you very much for reading Murder in the Churchyard! I had so much fun writing this story and I very much hope you enjoyed reading it. If you did, please consider leaving a review. Not only do reviews help other readers decide if Murder in the Churchyard is a book they might like to read but they also help me know what readers did, and did not enjoy, about my book.

If you would like to be amongst the first to know about my new releases, please join my monthly newsletter (you can do this via my website – details below)

I have also formed a Facebook group for fans of cozy mysteries. It's a place where we can chat about the books we've read, the things we like about cozies, any TV programmes in the cozy genre etc.. It is also the place where I will share what I'm writing, price drops, but most of all letting readers know about FREE ARCs that will be available (you can do this via my website – details below).

Thanks,
Catherine
www.catherinecoles.com

Printed in Great Britain
by Amazon